The chemistry had always been strong, one of the reasons why his abrupt ending of their relationship had hit her so hard.

The night before his trip to Milan, he'd made love to her the whole night through.

Sometimes she looked back and wondered how she'd survived it all.

The path she needed to take, half formulated in Xavi's office, had come more sharply into focus.

She would accept the arrogant bastard's proposal. Yes, she would marry him and let him use her shares to continue his role as chairman and CEO uncontested, and while he was merrily running the precious business that meant much more to him than she ever had, she would sell off her grandfather's villa and other assets and use the proceeds to buy up the other shares until *she* became the majority shareholder. She might even go into cahoots with the American sharks who'd already attempted a hostile takeover.

Whatever she did, *she* would be the one to oust him from his precious business and destroy his dreams the way he'd destroyed hers, and then she would eject him from her life once and for all.

Michelle Smart's love affair with books started when she was a baby and would cuddle them in her cot. A voracious reader of all genres, she found her love of romance established when she stumbled across her first Harlequin book at the age of twelve. She's been reading them—and writing them—ever since. Michelle lives in Northamptonshire, England, with her husband and two young smarties.

Books by Michelle Smart

Harlequin Presents

Innocent's Wedding Day with the Italian
Christmas Baby with Her Ultra-Rich Boss
Cinderella's One-Night Baby
Resisting the Bossy Billionaire
Spaniard's Shock Heirs

The Greek Groom Swap

The Forbidden Greek

The Diamond Club

Heir Ultimatum

Greek Rivals

Forgotten Greek Proposal
His Pregnant Enemy Bride
Greek Boss to Hate

Visit the Author Profile page
at Harlequin.com for more titles.

MARRIAGE MADE IN REVENGE

MICHELLE SMART

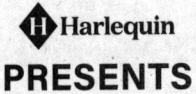

PRESENTS

If you purchased this book without a cover you should be aware that this book is stolen property. It was reported as "unsold and destroyed" to the publisher, and neither the author nor the publisher has received any payment for this "stripped book."

MIX
Paper | Supporting responsible forestry
FSC® C021394

ISBN-13: 978-1-335-21367-9

Marriage Made in Revenge

Copyright © 2026 by Michelle Smart

All rights reserved. No part of this book may be used or reproduced in any manner whatsoever without written permission.

Without limiting the exclusive rights of any author, contributor or the publisher of this publication, any unauthorized use of this publication to train generative artificial intelligence (AI) technologies is expressly prohibited. Harlequin also exercises their rights under Article 4(3) of the Digital Single Market Directive 2019/790 and expressly reserves this publication from the text and data mining exception.

This is a work of fiction. Names, characters, places and incidents are either the product of the author's imagination or are used fictitiously. Any resemblance to actual persons, living or dead, businesses, companies, events or locales is entirely coincidental.

For questions and comments about the quality of this book, please contact us at CustomerService@Harlequin.com.

TM and ® are trademarks of Harlequin Enterprises ULC.

Harlequin Enterprises ULC
22 Adelaide St. West, 41st Floor
Toronto, Ontario M5H 4E3, Canada
www.Harlequin.com

HarperCollins Publishers
Macken House, 39/40 Mayor Street Uppe
Dublin 1, D01 C9W8, Ireland
www.HarperCollins.com

Printed in Lithuania

MARRIAGE
MADE IN REVENGE

CHAPTER ONE

BETH GRANGER PULLED up outside the magnificent villa she hadn't set foot in since she was nineteen years old. All around her, people dressed in black were getting out of their cars and embracing each other as if they hadn't already spent the day embracing and pretending to mourn.

Through her rearview mirror, she watched the large black SUV with the tinted windows make its way through the gates, and closed her eyes.

Her heart was thumping hard enough for the ripples to make her motion-sick.

She didn't know if she could do this. All she wanted was to drive back to the airport and take the first flight home to England.

The day had been a million times harder than she'd anticipated. Beth hadn't been close to her grandfather, but he was her last biological link to her mother. For that fact alone, he deserved better than to have his only living relative spend his funeral with her mind and emotions concentrated on someone else.

She'd genuinely believed she was over Xavi. She'd seen him a number of times since their break-up at parties that had been held during duty visits to her grandfather. Those occasions had always been emotionally difficult, but sheer bloody-minded pride had forbidden her from letting Xavi see just how difficult it was for her to be under the same roof as him. She'd taken *fake it until you make it* to professional levels; so much so that the bastard genuinely thought they were on friendly terms.

The last thing she'd wanted or expected was to walk into the chapel of rest eight years after their ending and for her senses to pick him out of the vast crowd like she was *still* some kind of Xavi-homing pigeon. Luckily, so many people had gathered to pay their respects to Beth's grandfather that there hadn't been the time or opportunity for them to do more than nod an acknowledgement of greeting to each other. She'd done herself proud with that smile, making sure it was just the right side of solemn—it was a funeral after all—and friendly. Oh yes, she'd mastered the art of being friendly to the bastard.

She'd done herself even prouder when she'd sensed his stare on her throughout the service. She hadn't reacted to it at all. Not externally. She was less proud that she'd had to fight herself not to look back at him. She'd *ached* to look at him. Worse, she'd ached for him to come and sit with her and hold her to him.

She could only assume her grandfather's death had triggered something in her because it felt like she'd returned to the days when she'd struggled to even get out of bed. The urge to reverse out of the driveway, fly home and bury herself in bed with a large tub of chocolate ice cream was close to irresistible.

Her grandfather, for all his many faults, deserved better, and Xavi de la Rosa was not worth all the calories that came from comfort eating.

It was nearly over. All she had to do was get through the wake. One hour of small talk and then *adios*, Spain. Forever.

Pulling her compact out of her bag, she was disconcerted to find her hands trembling. She took a deep breath. The vain, prideful side of her nature would never allow Xavi to see her looking anything other than her best, so she reapplied her lip gloss and touched up her eyeliner as best she could before climbing out of the car. After straightening her dress, she blew her fringe out of her eyes, tucked a lock of hair behind an ear, elongated her neck and then put her best foot forward towards the villa she'd last been in the day Xavi had smashed her heart into pieces.

From his vantage point in the main open-plan living area of his family's villa, Xavi de la Rosa watched the curvy redhead swish through the reception room, stunningly understated in a calf-length flowing black shirt dress cinched at the waist with a thick black belt, and long, heeled black boots.

As always happened, his heart juddered in an echo of the first time he'd set eyes on her.

Eight years and she'd hardly changed at all. Every time he saw her, he marvelled at how well she'd matured into full-blown womanhood. Her long, thick red hair still shone gold under the sunlight, and she still had the same narrow face, crystal-clear green eyes, apple cheekbones and slightly square chin. Same snub nose and pixie ears, too. Her generous curves were more voluptuous, her hourglass figure one that people always took a second admiring look at.

The Beth Xavi had fallen for all those years ago had been a fun-loving eighteen-year-old who'd mesmerised him from the very first glance. She'd been quick-tempered but also quick to smile and even quicker to laugh, a hugger who was affectionate with everyone. It was a trait she'd never lost, and he watched her embrace everyone who approached her as if they were old friends when she only distantly knew a few of the hundreds of people gathered there. Those who'd never met her were naturally curious about Raul Belmonte's only living heir. Once the news broke about her inheritance, the whole of Spain would be curious about her, too.

She stepped away from an embrace with the flamboyant artistic director of an Italian fashion house, and for the first time since entering the de la Rosa villa, her stare glanced Xavi's. She smiled at him, and for a moment, barely the beat of a second, the connection between them was strong enough to touch. The beat broke when his mother pulled Beth into a tight embrace.

It was time to make his move.

The hairs on the nape of Beth's neck lifted. Her chest tightened.

He was heading towards her. She could feel it as she always did, and tightened her hold on her handbag.

'It's so lovely seeing you again,' she said to Mireia, Xavi's mother, in her best Spanish. 'Thank you for—' she couldn't think of the words to say, 'making all the arrangements,' and so settled for '—all this.' Meaning the funeral.

As her grandfather's only living relative, Beth should have been the one to arrange the funeral, but living in a different country and not knowing the first thing about Spanish funeral customs, she'd gratefully accepted Mireia's offer of organising everything, right down to opening her home for the wake. The de la Rosas had known Beth's grandfather a million times better than she had. Beth hadn't even known of his existence until her eighteenth birthday.

'Hello, Beth.'

Even though she'd braced herself for it, hearing that perfect English delivered in that rich, deep voice made her heart flip.

Keeping her features composed took more strength and concentration than all the other times she'd seen him since he broke her heart. Turning to face him, keeping that hard-fought composure drew reserves she hadn't known existed.

'Hello, Xavi,' she replied lightly, meeting the dark chocolate brown stare. 'You're looking well.'

The young man who'd swept her off her feet was now thirty-two and much changed. The cropped hair, almost the same dark chocolate colour of his eyes, was longer than he'd worn it when they were together, the gorgeous smooth face covered in a neat, dark beard. The changes suited him, as did the faint lines around his eyes and on his forehead. Even the black suit he wore looked effortlessly elegant on his tall, wiry frame. The bastard.

His wide, sensuous lips made the ghost of a smile before his large hands clasped her shoulders, and he leaned down to press a kiss to both of her cheeks.

There was no time for her to prepare herself or hold her breath before sensation zinged over her skin and she was engulfed in a scent so familiar and loved that everything inside her contracted.

Keeping his hands on her shoulders, he stepped back and studied her with a widening smile. 'You look incredible.'

Somehow, she managed a playful wiggle of her head. 'One does one's best… So, how are things? I imagine the last few days have been difficult for you.' Her grandfather had retired from the luxury brand conglomerate he'd founded with Xavi's grandfather three years ago. She'd attended his retirement party, had been there when he'd publicly entrusted his share of the company in Xavi's hands and expressed his full confidence in him to achieve great things for the Rosbel Group. She'd applauded like everyone else in attendance and congratulated Xavi with a smile and an embrace. She'd even kissed his cheek and resisted disinfecting her mouth until she was alone in a bathroom.

He'd been running the company single-handedly since, just as the bastard had always wanted. Her grandfather's death had made international news, the press descending on the Rosbel Group's headquarters in a frenzied determination to know what Raul Belmonte's death meant for the company.

His smile became rueful. 'Nothing I can't handle.'

'I'm sure.' It was only human emotions Xavi couldn't cope with.

'How about you? Are you keeping well in yourself?'

'Very much so.'

'That's good to hear.' The smile around his mouth faded, but the sparkle in his eyes didn't diminish at all. 'Can you spare me a few minutes of your time? There is something I need to discuss with you.'

Her stomach plummeting, she made a point of looking at her watch. 'I've got a flight to catch, so you'll have to make it quick.'

'I'll be as quick as I can, but it is best we speak in private.'

Her plummeting stomach now quivering, she raised an intrigued eyebrow. 'That sounds ominous.'

The lines around his eyes crinkled. 'Nothing ominous, I promise. It's to do with your grandfather's estate and the legacy he's left you.'

They were words to make her pause. 'What legacy?'

'That is what we need to discuss.'

'Shouldn't the lawyers be the ones to discuss it with me?'

'Trust me, it is better you hear it from me first.'

How she didn't punch him in the face for that she would never know.

Trust the man who'd promised to love her forever?

Trust the man who'd been her earth and her sun, and then broken her?

But Beth hadn't spent eight years carefully curating social media posts—Xavi had never stopped following her on them, his frequent 'likes' and comments proving he kept an eye on them—and turning Photoshop into her best friend for nothing, and she made another point of looking at her watch. 'I can give you ten minutes, and then I'm really sorry but I'll need to make a move.' She didn't need to make a move anywhere. Her flight home didn't take off for another six hours.

It was Xavi she wanted to escape; Xavi and this villa and all the memories tying together, memories making the past feel like she could touch it, and if she could touch it then she could feel it, and God help her if she ever had to feel any of that again.

'I'll be as concise as I can,' he promised in his shamefully excellent English. 'Walk in the garden with me?'

'I don't have sunscreen on,' she lied as a strong memory of falling asleep on the sprawling de la Rosa lawn beneath the shade of an olive tree and being woken by a kiss smashed through her. The de la Rosas had been having a family summer party, and Beth had got all sleepy after too much sangria. With voices floating in the distance, Xavi had woken her with a kiss and then silently brought her to orgasm with nothing but his hand.

It had tortured her imagining him doing that with the women who had come after her. Her third trip to Madrid after their break-up had been to celebrate the New Year with her grandfather. He'd taken her to a party thrown by one of Spain's leading art dealers, and the first person Beth had seen when they'd walked into the villa had been Xavi with a blonde bombshell attached to his arm. Beth had made a point of going over to them, throwing her arms around Xavi as if they were long-lost best friends and befriending the appendage. She'd kept her happy face going the whole night, dancing, drinking and making merry like everyone else. The next day she'd flown back to England, detoured to a supermarket on her way home, then sat in bed eating her weight in chocolate ice cream. It had taken her months to recover from the painful shock of seeing him so clearly happy with someone else. It was a shock Beth had never understood as she knew damned well he'd replaced her with that Ellen bitch days after breaking off his relationship with her.

'Let's talk in the study,' she suggested. That was one room they'd never done anything dirty in.

In their time together, they'd made love in every room of this sprawling villa. It had been a game to them, their own playful version of sex bingo. Only the occupied bedrooms had been off-limits. The only room they'd failed to christen and so get a full house in before Xavi had dumped her was the study, so at least there wouldn't be any sex memories to slap her around the face in it.

As soon as she crossed its threshold, though, and the door closed them inside the intimate space, Beth knew she'd made a mistake and cursed herself for lying about the sunscreen. They could have talked at the front of the villa by her hired car, and then she could have driven off, 'accidentally' screeching the wheels so he got a face full of gravel in the process.

Determined to give away nothing of her inner turmoil and to continue projecting the carefree image she so carefully curated on her social media feeds, she hitched her ample backside onto the highly polished mahogany desk and folded her arms loosely across her stomach rather than wrapping them in the tight hug she so desperately needed to hold herself with. She looked him in the eye with a smile. 'Well?'

Instead of telling her about her mysterious legacy, he strode to a cabinet, looked through its contents and pulled out a bottle of whisky and two crystal glasses. 'Drink? Or shall I have one of the staff make up a strawberry daiquiri for you?'

Beth's cocktail of choice. Her social media posts showed her enjoying them at regular intervals.

'Thank you, but I'm driving.'

'Very responsible,' he said drily, filling a glass for himself to the brim.

'Practising to be an alcoholic?' she asked with a grin she only managed by imagining herself throwing the whisky all over his ultra-expensive hand-tailored suit.

He raised the glass to her and drank half the contents. 'Dutch courage.'

'You are full of intrigue, *Señor de la Rosa*, but I've got a flight to catch so tell me about this legacy. Has he left me one of his paintings? Or maybe a car?' A thought made her blanch. 'Not Diego? I'm not allowed pets.' Not in her apartment building. And she had no garden. *Surely*, he wouldn't have left his Spanish Water Dog in her care? Surely, he'd have left him in his housekeeper Salma's care?

'He's left you the lot.'

She blinked, unsure of what she'd heard. 'He's left me a *pot*?'

'*The lot.* Everything. The villa and all its contents. All his cars and holiday homes. His personal helicopter and his shares in the business. Diego. Everything. It's all yours.'

She studied his serious face a long moment before bursting into laughter. 'That's a good one. You nearly had me going for a minute. Go on, tell me, what's he really left me?'

Not a flicker of amusement crossed his face. 'Your grandfather has left you everything, Beth.'

Still grinning widely, she shook her head. 'Not a chance. He took great delight in reminding me of his intentions for his estate every time I visited him—he was leaving his Rosbel Group shares to your family and everything else to charity.'

'He kept saying that in the hope it would entice you into changing your mind about working for the company. He never seriously intended to disinherit you—it was just a threat, a ploy for you to give in and comply with his wishes. You were his only living heir, and that meant everything to him.'

She laughed to cover how unsettled she was with the whole situation and jumped off the desk. Snatching the glass from Xavi's hand, she tipped the remaining whisky down her throat.

Beth hated whisky, but right then she needed something to cut through the effect of being in an enclosed space with Xavi and the shock of what he'd just told her.

The hefty measure burning her throat wasn't enough, and she refilled the glass and drank it in three swallows.

'I thought you were driving,' Xavi said, eyebrow risen.

'Stuff it, I'll get a taxi. After all, you've just told me I'm rich.' And with that, she burst into another peal of laughter.

Rich? Possibly the biggest understatement in the world.

Beth's mother, Lorena, had died in childbirth. Beth had been raised by her father and her grandparents. Her childhood had been happy. She'd missed having a mother, but in a very abstract, curious way. She couldn't miss her as a mother because she'd never known her, but she'd been filled with curiosity about her. Everything she'd learned about her had painted a picture of a fierce but happy, loving Spanish woman who loved to dance and run barefoot. A free spirit, much like Beth.

One thing, though, that Beth had never been told about was her mother's family. The impression she'd been given growing up was that her mother didn't have any family.

This impression had been a lie engineered by her father. She'd only learned the truth on her eighteenth birthday when an elderly Spanish man knocked on their door and introduced himself as her grandfather.

Lorena, it transpired, had been estranged from her father since her late teens. Her own mother had left him when Lorena was only twelve. When Lorena had moved to England, she'd never seen either of her parents again.

Beth's father had respected his dead wife's feelings

and had refused to let her father have any involvement in their daughter's life until she was eighteen and old enough to make her own judgement about him.

Learning of her Spanish grandfather's existence had come as a huge shock. A lifetime of barely satisfied curiosity about her mother, and all along she'd had a grandfather? To then learn her Spanish grandmother had died only two years earlier...

That had been a huge blow, but she'd swallowed her hurt and anger at the lies of omission from her father because he was her father and she loved him, and even through her hurt, she'd known he'd acted for what he thought was the best. Her English grandparents had felt compelled to go along with his decision on the matter.

The second shock Beth had received that fateful day was learning her grandfather was rich.

Not just rich but stupendously rich. Raul Belmonte was co-owner of the Rosbel Group, one of the wealthiest companies in Europe, making Beth's grandfather one of the richest men in Europe.

His wealth, though, had meant nothing to her, not when she was gazing at the face of the only living biological link to the mother she'd never known. Her desire to know him had been strong, but she'd known before she agreed to spend a summer with him that he wasn't the fluffy, kindly old man he was trying to portray himself to her as. After all, her mother had been estranged from him for a reason, and just because he'd not been allowed to see her didn't mean he couldn't have helped her father out financially or put some money aside for her.

Those thoughts weren't motivated by greed but by comparing him to her paternal grandparents, who'd taken their son and his motherless newborn baby into their small home and helped raise their grandchild. On the day her super-rich grandfather presented himself to her like a long-lost unicorn, they'd presented her with a bank statement worth four thousand pounds. It was money they'd invested over the years in a child-saver bank account for her, money they'd hoped would be useful as she stepped into adulthood. Her grandfather probably earned that amount—if not more—in interest on an hourly basis.

The months she'd spent with her grandfather in Madrid confirmed her worst fears as to the kind of man he was. If not for the gorgeous Spaniard who'd swept her off her feet, Beth would have flown back to England within days.

The *ifs* were many. If her grandfather hadn't decided to invite his business partner, Ferdinand de la Rosa, and Ferdinand's family to a dinner party to show off his granddaughter on her second night in his home, Beth would never have met Xavi. If Ferdinand hadn't been grooming his grandson to take over the running of the Rosbel Group, and Raul determined to teach Beth everything about the business, too, Beth and Xavi wouldn't have spent so much time together.

By the end of her first week in Madrid, she'd been smitten, and so she'd stayed. By the time autumn morphed into winter, she was back in England with a broken heart and shattered dreams.

'Do you understand what this means, Beth?'

She blinked herself back to the present and to the man responsible for her broken heart. 'Yes. It means I have a dog.'

Diego had been her grandfather's only real redeeming feature. He'd doted on the soppy Spanish Water Dog.

'It means you and I are now business partners. As you know, my grandfather retired five years ago and put the de la Rosa shares under my control—I've since bought my family out, so the shares are mine alone. When your grandfather retired, he entrusted his shares into my safekeeping and gave me the power to act and vote on his behalf. His death means those shares are now yours to do with as you wish. We each own thirty per cent of the company.'

Beth thought about the glamorous Rosbel Group headquarters in the heart of Madrid's business district and all the luxury brands under its control and the stonking value of it all. Thought, too, of all her grandfather's other assets, and shook her head in growing disbelief.

She'd never believed for a second he would leave her any of it. In the months Beth had spent working for the company, it had been like a war zone between them, ending in a screaming match when Beth had taken one too many long lunches for her grandfather's liking. Her grandfather had shouted that if she wasn't prepared to take the business seriously and learn her way around it and take her rightful place within it, he would leave his shares to the de la Rosas and everything else to charity. She'd shouted at him to go ahead and then refused to set foot in the headquarters again.

That was another of those *ifs*. If she hadn't been head over heels in love with Xavi, she would have flown straight home and probably never seen her grandfather again. Instead, she'd continued living with him, and slowly they'd thawed and forgiven each other.

She hadn't wanted his money or to be groomed to run an empire and would never have agreed to spend the summer with him if she'd known that had been his end game. She'd wanted a grandfather, something he'd come to accept, even if he didn't have a clue how to be a grandfather, but he'd been the last link to her mother, and that had been enough for Beth to learn to forgive the sense that he was hiding something fundamental about himself from her and his many, many flaws. She thought it had been the same for him, too.

'If we combine our shares like our grandfathers did, we retain control of the Rosbel Group,' Xavi said, pulling her out of yet another reverie.

She met his dark brown stare. It seemed impossible that the man who exuded such warmth could be so cold and cruel and so careless with another's heart. 'I take it you want me to entrust my shares with you like my grandfather did?' As if she'd trust him with *anything*.

'Whoever has the majority holding has the controlling interest. I've already fought off one hostile takeover—an American corporation with a fifteen per cent stake. I hear its ringleader's in financial trouble now, but I have no doubt that your grandfather's death means they or others like them will be on manoeuvres again soon.'

She downed the last of the whisky. 'So you *do* want me to entrust my shares with you.'

'In a fashion.' He refilled her glass and filled a glass for himself.

'What kind of fashion? Do you want to buy them?' He could want all he liked. Hell would freeze over before she handed him a single share of the business he'd chosen over her.

'Only if you refuse my proposition.'

'Which is?'

A hint of caution came into his voice. 'I want you to promise to hear my reasoning.'

She shrugged. 'That's fine.'

He studied her long enough for her skin to prickle and her heart to pound harder. 'Just hear me out and then take the time to think about it before giving me your answer. Take all the time you need.'

The prickles on her skin were growing, a sense of dread and anticipation uncoiling in her stomach. She took another drink to calm it and nodded. 'I can do that.'

He leaned back against the cabinet, drank some whisky and said, 'I want us to marry.'

CHAPTER TWO

Xavi watched Beth's reaction closely. Other than the slightest twitching of her lips, she gave nothing away... not unless you counted the sudden loss of colour on her face. Although the knuckles of the fingers holding her glass had whitened, too, nothing suggested she was about to throw the glass at him.

He would never forget the sound of shattering glass in the moments before he'd kicked open the door of the bathroom she'd locked herself in. He'd found the tiled floor covered with shards of glass and clumps of wax from the scented candles she'd thrown on it, but his fear that she'd been hurting herself went unrealised. By the time he'd smashed the door in, all the emotions driving her to destroy his bathroom had worked their way out of her system.

Beautiful face red and blotchy through crying, she'd looked him in the eye, apologised for the mess she'd made, and with quiet dignity walked out of his life.

Two years passed before he next saw her in the flesh at her grandfather's eightieth birthday. She'd embraced him warmly and even made a joke about the state she'd left his bathroom in. He'd been relieved, but also strangely disconcerted. It wasn't that he'd wanted histrionics or a glass of water thrown in his face, but to find he'd meant so little to her that she could treat their break-up like a joke had thrown him.

The tendons of her neck stretching, she jerked her head, indicating for him to explain his reasoning.

'I appreciate my proposition must come as a surprise.'

Her face scrunched up, and she matter-of-factly said, 'Just a tiny bit considering we once spent a whole evening discussing the kind of wedding we wanted, and then weeks later you dumped me.'

Chest and stomach wincing simultaneously, he inclined his head in agreement. 'I never did apologise for the way I ended things with you, did I.'

She waved an airy hand and rolled her eyes. 'Xavi, it was eight years ago.'

Eight years and yet he still remembered their time together so vividly that it could have been days ago. He doubted it was the same for her. For all her words of love, Beth had got over him pretty damned quickly, something he knew he had no right to resent. He had no right, either, to feel jealousy whenever she posted photos on social media of her raising a glass with a group of friends that usually had equal numbers of men and women. Whenever he made the occasional comment to her posts, she always reacted, whether with a thumbs-up or a heart or with a witty remark that made his mouth smile and his heart hurt.

He made his mouth smile now. 'I'm just saying that I appreciate my clumsy way of ending things will make it harder for you to take my proposal seriously.'

She smiled. He'd always loved Beth's smile. Her top lip was just the slightest bit fuller than the bottom one, and when she smiled her mouth formed an upside-down heart. 'Forget the past and tell me your reasoning. If nothing else, I'm curious.'

'For one, it better protects the business and both our interests in it,' he answered steadily. For all her smiles, there was a sharpness in Beth's stare that told him she would detect any hint of bullshit.

'How?'

'Your grandfather's death has already increased speculation and scrutiny of the business, and it will encourage the sharks to start circling again. Marriage will allow us to pool our shares the same way our grandfathers did and allow me to continue running the Rosbel Group without outside interference and make us both a lot of money—profits have increased significantly since I took control. Us marrying gives certainty to the tens of thousands of people we employ around the world and gives certainty to the financial markets, too.'

'Wow, you really know how to make a girl feel special with *that* reasoning for marriage.'

Refusing to allow himself to remember how he'd woken one morning to find her already awake and gazing at him and how he'd said, 'We *are* going to marry, aren't we?' he pulled a rueful smile. 'You could entrust them to me or I could buy the shares from you, and the effect would be the same, but marrying me protects you, too.'

Her eyes narrowed. 'Hmm...how have you worked that out?'

'You're a very wealthy woman now, Beth. The sharks won't just circle the business, they'll be out circling you, too.'

'Why would the sharks know about me?'

'It will soon be public knowledge that Raul left everything to you.'

'Not if no one tells them.'

Xavi knew she wasn't naive enough to believe that. 'Your grandfather was one of the richest men in Europe. Whoever he left his wealth to would make the news—that he's left everything to the granddaughter who didn't want it adds to the story. That his granddaughter is beautiful by anyone's standards will have the press salivating. Every shark and chancer in the western hemisphere will want to take their chances with you. Once the news breaks, you will find yourself unable to trust anyone you don't already know. I can help you navigate this world.'

'That doesn't require marriage.'

'Agreed. But it will make it easier for me to protect you.'

She laughed and pulled a face. 'I don't need protecting.'

'You will, very soon, and you are not prepared for it.'

'Again, protection doesn't require marriage. I can buy an army to keep me safe.'

'Beth, you will never be able to trust another man again. That is your new reality. Always you will wonder if it's you they want or your money, and those suspicions will not go away if you have the children you always wanted with them.'

For the first time, he detected a flash of emotion in the crystal-clear green eyes. 'But you expect me to trust you?'

He dragged his fingers through his hair and forced air into his lungs. This was do or die. If Beth refused to marry him, the business would never be safe from the predators. 'I have always hated myself for hurting you, but if I had to make that choice again, I would make it without hesitation because the business has to come first. I lost sight of that when I was with you. I lost my focus and made some stupid but dangerous errors that would have cost the business dearly if our grandfathers hadn't picked up on them. It dented their confidence in me and made me see how close I'd come to destroying everything they'd built. My life and focus had been all on you when it should have been on the business, and I needed to switch it around and prove their confidence in my abilities to run the Rosbel Group wasn't misplaced.'

Pretty lips trembled as she looked him up and down before they pulled into a tight smile. 'That's a lot of words to reiterate that you chose the business over me.'

A statement he could not and would not deny. 'Beth, since my father died, all I've wanted is to step into the shoes he was unable to fill and take over the running of the Rosbel Group—you know this. My grandfather wanted to retire twenty years ago, but he couldn't have predicted his only son would die at such a young age.' Xavi's father had died when he was fourteen. Not even billions in wealth could stop cancer's advance. 'That's why our grandfathers' bond remained so strong—they both lost a child. They both lost the heirs they expected to take the company forward.'

'My grandfather lost his daughter long before she died.'

'Yes, which is why it was so important that I stepped up to the mark. I always knew it had to be me. I was the only family member left from either side of the partnership with the aptitude and willingness to do it.'

Like Beth's mother, Xavi's father had been an only child. Xavi's sisters had never had any interest in the business, one growing up to be an archaeologist, the other a human rights lawyer.

As a child, he'd happily imagined himself working with his father, whom he'd hero-worshipped. His father would take over the running of the Rosbel Group, and then one day, Xavi would step into his father's shoes.

He'd had no idea fate had such a cruel trick planned for his family.

'I know I ended things abruptly with you,' he continued, 'but I saw it like ripping off a plaster—once I knew I had to end it, I knew it was better to make a clean break.'

Pressing her crystal glass to her breasts, she arched an eyebrow. 'Better for whom?'

He would not look at her breasts. 'For both of us. I was too young for marriage back then. We both were. Hell, I was twenty-four and fresh from six years of back-to-back university degrees, and you'd only just turned nineteen. What were we thinking, talking about marriage and children when we were barely adults ourselves?'

'I completely agree.'

'You do?'

'Absolutely. I was young and foolish and believed in love at first sight, whereas what we had, if we're thinking logically, was more of an instant lust thing than love.' She gave another smile. 'If it meant what we both believed it to mean while we were living it, neither of us would have moved on so quickly.'

'For sure.' He would not allow himself to remember the sensation of his heart ripping when he'd seen a post of Beth beaming widely with her cheek pressed to another man's at a New Year's Eve party months after he'd ended their relationship. 'And now we both have eight years more experience of life and the world at large. We're ready to take that step now. You're the only woman I've ever trusted—what I said about sharks and chancers circling you comes from experience. You're the only woman I've been with that I had complete certainty was with me for me and not for my money and connections, and you can have that same trust and certainty with me. We were good together, Beth, and there is no reason to suppose we can't be good together again, and this time we're old enough and mature enough to make it work.'

There was a flash in the green eyes that had been studying him so intently. 'You say all that about trust... if it wasn't for the shares now being mine, would you be asking me to marry you?'

He returned the intensity of the stare. 'I've never stopped caring about you.'

'That isn't what I asked.'

'I know, but if I didn't care, I wouldn't be suggesting it. I couldn't marry someone I feel nothing for. I'm ready for marriage now and ready for children, and who better to do all that with than the other half of the Rosbel Group? Marry me and you will have the confidence that your fortune is safe because I will only ever do what's best for the business, and I will keep you safe, too, and always act in your best interests. It is a perfectly logical move for both of us... Unless you are already in a relationship you haven't gone public with?'

Her pretty little nose lifted into the air. 'I'm not officially attached to anyone at the moment if that's what you mean.'

His heart thumped at this confirmation. 'And neither am I.'

She took a step closer to him and lifted her chin, the clear eyes ringed with sweeping, thickly mascaraed lashes studying him even harder. 'I always assumed you would end up with Ellen.'

His head reared back in surprise. 'I wouldn't marry that bunny boiler.'

Ellen had been a part of Xavi's old social circle, a hanger-on who'd wormed her way into his group of friends during his years studying in England. She'd been the most predatory woman he'd ever had the misfortune to know. She'd made no bones about her attraction to Xavi—an attraction in no way reciprocated—and when Beth had come on the scene had been so snide and nasty to her that he'd taken to avoiding gatherings she'd be at to protect Beth from her.

'So she didn't finally lure you into her bed after we split?'

For the first time in their exchange, he hesitated before answering, remembering the time Ellen had sent him unsolicited nude selfies with the message: *Look what you're missing out on.* Up to that point, Beth had felt quite sorry for her, arguing that she must be lonely and insecure to be so bitchy and behave so outrageously. One look at those pictures and the message, and she'd wanted to storm to Ellen's home and rip her hair out.

'No.'

There was another flickering in the green depths, her lips making the faintest of twitches. 'Okay,' she eventually said, tilting her head as she drained the last of her whisky. 'I'll think about marrying you.'

'You will consider it seriously?'

'Yes.' She stretched her arm to put her empty glass on the cabinet. 'But before I start thinking about it, I think we need to establish something first.'

'Which is?'

'This.' Without any warning, she'd closed the gap between them, risen onto her toes to wrap her arms around his neck and pull him closer, and then her soft lips captured his.

Since Xavi had been given the news of Raul's death, his thoughts had been consumed twofold: with retaining his control of the business and with the certain knowledge that he would be seeing Beth again. It wasn't until he'd woken that morning, though, that the two strains of his thoughts had converged and the big picture had made itself clear.

Everything he'd told her of his reasoning for marriage had been the truth. The biggest truth was that the

Rosbel Group was *his* and he would do anything to protect it and protect his control of it, and so he'd concentrated all his energies on what he needed to say, instinct telling him this was his one shot at getting Beth's agreement, and clamped down on all the physical reactions being in her presence had unleashed. He'd suppressed the zing flowing through his veins, blocked his senses to the heady scent of her perfume, refused to allow his mind to strip her naked or remember the weight of her breasts in his hands...

One press of her lips to his, and the eight years they'd spent apart melted away along with all thoughts of the Rosbel Group.

There was no hesitation in her kiss. Her fingers scraped through his hair and her tongue slipped into his mouth, and then she was devouring him with a hungry boldness that sent his senses reeling under a blizzard of sensation.

Dios, he'd forgotten how much he'd missed her. Missed *this*. Missed the magic that he'd singularly failed to replicate with anyone else.

Revelling in the softness of Beth's lips and the warm silkiness of her tongue, Xavi set the glass in his hand onto the cabinet and then wrapped his arms tightly around her, kissing her back with matching hunger. *Dios*, she tasted even better than he remembered, and he deepened the kiss until her breasts were crushed against his chest and they were nothing but two tightly locked bodies and fused faces.

It was Beth who pulled away first.

Keeping her hands linked around his neck, she drew

back to gaze at him with dilated pupils. Her cheeks were flush and there was a breathless quality to her voice as she murmured, 'Well, that's answered my question.'

'What question was that?' he asked huskily.

'Whether the chemistry is still there...' She brought her mouth back to his. 'Let's do that again.'

Lips and bodies crashing back together, the thrills that raged through him were strong enough to melt bone.

This was why there had been no magic with anyone since Beth. Xavi didn't feel his desire for her just in his loins but in the whole of his being. Theirs was a chemical formula impossible to replicate.

Squeezing the succulent bottom that was as soft and pillowy as her glorious breasts, he gathered the skirt of her dress; would have steered her to the desk and lifted her onto it if she hadn't broken the kiss again and gently pushed at his chest in an unspoken gesture to say their chemical experiment was over.

His breaths as heavy as the thumps of his heart and the weight of his erection, he gazed into Beth's desire-laden eyes and didn't know whether to laugh or groan when she blew her fringe out of her eyes, staggered to the desk to grab her bag and then staggered to the door.

Arousal coursed so strongly through him that it took a moment to speak. 'Where are you going?'

The breathless quality in her voice deepened. 'Somewhere to think.' She turned back to face him and lifted her chin. 'I'll let you know of my decision soon.'

'How soon?'

After gathering her gorgeous autumn-leaved hair

onto the top of her head, she let it fall as she smiled knowingly. 'As soon as I've made it.'

Another knowing smile, and she slipped out of the study, shutting the door quietly behind her.

Xavi stared at the closed door for an age and then shook his head and laughed, more with relief than anything else.

Considering he'd half anticipated a punch in the face, he'd say that had gone damned well.

Beth had given him a fair hearing, which, despite the friendly nature of their relationship since their split, was more than he'd expected. More than he deserved if he was being honest with himself. She hadn't thrown anything at him. And she'd kissed him… *Dios*, how she had kissed him.

He wondered how many other men she'd kissed with such boldness, then cut the thought off at the knees with much-practised precision. He'd been Beth's first, and if he had his way, he would be her last, a thought that was almost as satisfying as securing his control of the Rosbel Group.

All the years spent apart from her had been with the hovering thought that one day the time would be right to bring Beth back into his life. Now was that time. All the things that had driven him to end things the first time no longer existed; the dangerous power Beth had had over him that had driven him to forget his responsibilities to the business now muted.

If she agreed to marry him, he had full confidence he could keep her compartmentalised in the way he'd never succeeded before.

Draining the last of his whisky, he came close to allowing himself the luxury of imagining Beth giving her agreement. But only close.

The only thing predictable about Beth Granger was her unpredictability.

Beth waited at the de la Rosas electric gates for her taxi and searched on her phone for a hotel. She'd sort out her hire car later. There were other things to do first. Things that had to take priority.

By the time her taxi turned up, she'd booked herself into a reasonably priced, superbly located hotel with decent reviews. Twenty minutes later, she was striding into its reception and being given the key to her room.

The room itself was clean, the bed large and comfortable. Most importantly, it had a multitude of pillows. She unzipped her boots, yanked them off and chucked them onto the floor, then crawled under the duvet, put her face on one of the pillows and pulled another two over her head, sandwiching herself in them.

Only then, knowing her screams would be muffled, did she open her vocal cords.

She screamed and raged until her throat was raw, and then she sat up, grabbed another pillow, got on her knees and started battering it with her fists. Imagining it was Xavi's face, she punched the pillow so hard and for so long that her knuckles stung.

She wished she could cry; would give anything to cauterise her pain with the release of tears. Not that tears cauterised anything, but they allowed emotions to be purged, even if only for a short while.

Beth hadn't been able to cry since the ocean of tears that had fallen when she'd miscarried her baby.

Xavi's baby.

The baby she had desperately wanted and loved with the whole of her being from the moment the pregnancy test had confirmed she was carrying his child.

She'd waited until he'd gone on a five-day work trip to Milan—their grandfathers had forbidden Beth from going with him—before taking the pregnancy test. She'd only been a couple of days late for her period and hadn't wanted to build Xavi's hopes up for nothing.

The rush of joy at the positive sign was like nothing she'd felt in her life, and she'd hugged her secret tightly to herself until he'd returned. She'd wanted to tell him to his face and see the joy on it.

Already practically living in the de la Rosa villa with him, she'd been waiting in his bedroom for his return from his trip, too excited about what was to come to think too hard that he'd been too busy that week for anything but short conversations and that he'd barely messaged her.

He'd stepped into the bedroom. One look at his face and the spring in her legs to bound over to him and tell him their wonderful news had turned to lead.

Xavi had thought taking the ripping-a-plaster-off approach the best way to end it? Well, he should have tried being the human that plaster had been ripped off of.

After six months of bliss, Xavi had run his fingers through his hair and curtly delivered his obviously prepared words. 'I'm sorry, Beth, but we need to end things. Neither of us is ready for marriage and I've been neglecting my responsibilities with the business when you know it has to be my priority. We've gone too far too fast and now we need to put the brakes on it.'

She'd never known such naked fear existed until she heard those words.

At her blank, open-mouthed stare, he'd jammed his hands into his pockets and ruefully added, 'It doesn't have to be forever. I hope we can part as friends because I'll always care for you and will always be there if you need me, but as things stand, I need to concentrate on the business. I owe my father and our grandfathers that.'

There had been an implacability to him, an emotional switch-off that had made him seem like a stranger, and she'd gazed at him in a strange state of petrified confusion and perfect understanding.

Xavi was an all-or-nothing man. He threw himself into whatever he set his mind to, and when he made up his mind about something, nothing could change it. He'd thrown himself into his love for her, but now the switch had been turned off. If he wanted Beth out of his life, nothing would change that.

That hadn't stopped her from trying when the shell shock gave way to hysteria, but the more she'd pleaded with him to change his mind, the more intractable he'd become. Hysteria had given way to pain-fuelled rage, and she'd locked herself in the bathroom and smashed anything she could get her hands on until the rage had given way to fear that if she didn't get a grip on herself, she would harm their baby.

It was thoughts of their baby that had made foolish hope spring alive and fill her. She just needed to wait for him to come to his senses because there was no way he meant it. Sure, Xavi never changed his mind when on a set course, but wasn't he changing the set course of their relationship? He was having cold feet or something like it, but in a few days or weeks he'd realise what a terrible mistake he'd made and beg her to come back to him, and then she'd forgive him and tell him about the baby and they'd all live happily ever after.

She'd gone back to her grandfather's full of misplaced hope. Five days later she'd sobbed her heart out for the final time in her bathroom, crippled with the pain of missing Xavi and crippled with abdominal pains she wouldn't wish on her worst enemy, not even that Ellen bitch.

That Ellen bitch who'd sent Beth a photo of Xavi sleeping in Ellen's bed just three days after Xavi had ended their relationship. She'd even location and time-stamped it for good measure.

Xavi had kicked Beth out of his life and days later jumped into the bed of the woman who'd spent their entire relationship practically stalking him and doing everything she could to lure him away from her, and barely two hours ago the bastard had barefaced lied about it. She'd have thought more of him—going from a base of zero, that wouldn't take much—if he'd admitted it.

And now he seriously thought she would agree to marry him and have his babies? Was he really so arrogant that he believed she'd forgiven him for so coldly throwing her away for the business? Did he really believe her friendliness the few times they'd seen each other and her breezy replies to his messages over the years were signs of her moving on rather than her pride demanding she pick herself up and prove she could live a good, fulfilling life without him just so he'd never know the depth of the agony he'd put her through?

She'd believed in him so strongly. Believed he was fundamentally good and true.

She should have known better. Hadn't her own father proved even the best of men could lie when he'd let her spend the first eighteen years of her life believing her mother had no living relatives? She should have known better than to expect more of Xavi, so more fool her. And more fool her for having a heart and body that hadn't learned their lessons well enough and still filled with longing for him.

She could still taste him on her tongue and feel the sensation in her breasts where they'd crushed against his chest. She could still feel the essence of Xavi flowing through her bloodstream, and she *despised* him for it.

Her kiss had been calculated. She'd wanted— needed—to prove to him that he wasn't the one in control and prove to herself that she'd matured enough to control her desires and not just be a slave to Xavi's.

By the time she'd pulled away the second time, her control had hung by a thread.

The chemistry between them had always been strong, one of the reasons why his abrupt ending of their relationship had hit her so hard. The night before his trip to Milan, he'd made love to her the whole night through.

Sometimes she looked back and wondered how she'd survived it all.

After swallowing hard, she pulled air into her lungs and stopped battering the poor, blameless pillow. The path she needed to take, half formulated in Xavi's office, had come more sharply into focus.

Throwing herself backwards, Beth spread her arms across the mattress, gazed up at the ceiling and concentrated all her thoughts and emotions.

She would accept the arrogant bastard's proposal. Yes, she would marry him and let him use her shares to continue his role as chairman and CEO uncontested, and while he was merrily running the precious business that meant much more to him than she ever had, she would sell off her grandfather's villa and other assets and use the proceeds to buy up the other shares until *she* became the majority shareholder. She might even go into cahoots with the American sharks who'd already attempted a hostile takeover.

Whatever she did, *she* would be the one to oust him from his precious business and destroy his dreams the way he'd destroyed hers, and then she would eject him from her life once and for all.

And then maybe, just maybe, she'd be able to move on from the invisible hold Xavi had kept her trapped in these past eight years and find a man deserving of her love.

CHAPTER THREE

Xavi's eyes snapped open to pitch black. His phone was ringing. He groped his bedside table until his hand fell on it.

Bringing it to his face, his heart slammed into his ribs and all sleepiness fell away when he saw the name on the screen.

'This is an unexpected pleasure,' he murmured. He'd thought she would make him wait a minimum of a week just to play with his mind.

'I'll marry you.'

He expelled a long breath and smiled. 'That is the best news a man could be woken to at two in the morning. I assume you timed it deliberately?'

'Naturally.'

'You always knew how to keep me on my toes.' And always in a good way. One particular memory stuck in his mind of Beth flopping onto her back after making love and deciding she wanted to go for a drive. It had been three in the morning. Thinking she just wanted to take it for a spin, he'd thrown some clothes on, indulgently given her the keys to his sports car and jumped in the passenger seat beside her. She'd put the soft top down, turned the music up and hit the accelerator. Three hours later, they'd been sat on La Malvarrosa beach eating churros and watching the sun rise.

Their impulsive trip had resulted in him missing a board meeting and being on the receiving end of his grandfather's anger and disapproval for the first time.

There was a long pause. 'Xavi, are you sure you want to do this? I'm not the Beth you remember. I haven't spent eight years in a silo. Things have happened that have shaped me.'

'What things?'

'Things I will tell you about when the time is right. I just need to be certain you understand that you won't be marrying the Beth of old.'

He laughed. 'You're still Beth, but I already know you're not the Beth of old, and I know we're going to have to get to know each other again, but *mi vida*, that kiss we shared proved the spark that was always there still lives.'

There was another long silence before she murmured, 'Okay, on your head be it. Don't say I didn't try to warn you.'

He laughed again. *Dios*, it felt good to laugh. It felt even better to know he'd soon have Beth back in his bed. The buzz in his veins since their kiss wasn't even close to abating. Just to imagine her head on the pillow next to his and her gorgeous red hair fanned over it made the buzz tighten and thicken in anticipation. 'Where are you? I'll send my driver for you.'

'Let him sleep,' she dismissed lightly. 'I need to go home and sort things out in England, but if you meet me at my grandfather's villa after breakfast, we can get the ball rolling for our wedding before I leave.'

He sighed and then grinned at his impatience. Just five minutes ago, he'd been asleep and expecting to wait days longer for her answer. If she'd said no, he'd have been back to fighting wars to retain his control of the Rosbel Group. Beth's agreement meant that fight was won *and* he had her back in his life.

Dios, all he'd thought about since their kiss was how good the sex had been between them. All their years apart, he'd forbidden himself from thinking about it, but now he was free to let the memories unleash and remember how incredible it had been between them. To break apart from her, he'd needed those days in Milan without her sexy, distracting presence to enable him to think clearly, had needed to block the receptors in his brain from switching on once he was back in his bedroom delivering the words he knew would break her heart.

The blocked receptors were back in full working order, and very soon, once she'd wrapped up her affairs in England, she'd be back in his bed permanently, and they could make up for all the lost time between them.

'I will get my team on it… How long are you going to make me wait to be my wife?'

She laughed, that old infectious, joyful sound that had never failed to bring a smile to his face. 'I'm happy to marry as soon as it can be arranged.'

'That makes me very happy.'

The tone of her voice changed slightly. 'I do need to ask a favour of you.'

'Anything.'

'Would you mind sorting out all the taxes and stuff on my grandfather's estate? I know it's all different to how it works in England and I wouldn't have a clue where to start.'

'Your grandfather named me as his executor, so consider it done.'

'Thank you.'

'*De nada.* What time tomorrow?'

'Nine?'

'That works for me.'

'Great. I'll see you then.'

'Sweet dreams, *mi vida.*'

Beth threw her phone across the hotel room floor and grabbed furiously at her hair.

The lying bastard! How dare he call her by that endearment?

Mi vida? My life? More like my *expendable* life.

Well, now it was Xavi who was expendable; Xavi who was going to learn how it felt to lose the most important thing in his life and for his life and dreams to be ripped apart.

By the time Beth was finished with Xavi de la Rosa, he would hate her every bit as much as she hated him.

It was hard to feel hate for someone when you walked into a villa and found them sitting around a dining room table looking all sexy in a dapper navy blue suit, pale blue shirt and thick checked silver tie, and with a large brown Spanish Water Dog on their lap, gazing at them adoringly whilst having the undersides of their ears rubbed.

Beth supposed it proved that dogs could be as stupid as humans. She'd once been as big a sucker for affection from Xavi as Diego. Still, it gave her perverse pleasure when Diego took one look at her from beneath the shaggy mane of curly hair on his head and jumped off Xavi's lap to charge over and run around her like she was his personal maypole.

'He likes you,' Xavi observed.

'He likes everyone.'

'Yes, but he *really* likes you. He clearly has excellent taste.'

'Clearly,' she agreed, laughing lightly, biting back the comment that if Diego really did have excellent taste, he wouldn't have given affection to Xavi. She would make sure to give the dog a stern warning of the danger of showing affection to Xavi when she was next alone with him.

To buy herself time to compose herself from all the memories that had started slamming into her before she'd even walked through the villa's front door and the slamming of her heart at the first glimpse of Xavi, she crouched down to cuddle Diego, taking much-needed comfort from his soft warmth.

This was the home the mother she'd never known had grown up in, the villa Beth had first walked into as an unworldly eighteen-year-old hoping to forge a relationship with the grandfather she'd never known. The villa she'd met Xavi in. The villa they'd made love in every room of except her grandfather's bedroom.

Even this dining room came prefilled with memories. Xavi had lifted her onto the sideboard dancing in her eye line, and taken her with such exquisiteness that she'd had to bite into his shoulder to stop her cries of ecstasy sounding through to the other rooms.

The room directly above this dining room was the bathroom she'd sobbed in when she'd miscarried their baby.

Still fussing over Diego, she forced herself to meet Xavi's warm brown stare and willed her racing pulses to settle. 'You know he's going to have to live with us?'

His lips curved. She imagined he'd carried that smug, self-satisfied smile since she'd agreed to his proposal.

He thought he had his future mapped out to his exact specifications. Let him enjoy the delusion while it lasted.

'I'd assumed as much.'

'I hope your home's not got too many valuables at low heights. Diego still behaves like a puppy at times.'

He stretched his long legs out and hooked his ankles together. 'I will get my staff to Diego-proof it.'

'Where do you live now? I assume you don't live in the family home anymore?' When she'd met him, he'd not long returned to Madrid after six years studying in England. Back then, it had thrilled her to think he'd lived only forty miles from her home in the heart of England.

There was the slightest hesitation. 'In Salamanca.'

She only just managed to stop herself from visibly blanching.

Xavi had once taken her shopping in Madrid's Salamanca district. The nineteenth-century neighbourhood oozed charm, glamour and beauty, and for Beth it had been love at first sight. So smitten had she been that when Xavi suggested buying a home for them there, she'd thrown her arms around his neck and kissed his face off.

'Oh, right,' she said as if she hadn't just had another knife plunged into her heart, and tried desperately to think of something light-hearted to add to cover the coldness of her shock.

When they'd been together, Xavi had been making plans to buy a place of his own. *Their* own. She was supposed to have moved into that place with him. In Salamanca. Moved into it and made a family of their own in it.

'What about your sisters?' she ended up plumping for. 'The last time I spoke to Carlota, she was still living at home…when she's not off on one of her archaeological digs, that is, but I haven't spoken to Blanca in years.'

Blanca was the human rights lawyer sister. Beth liked her very much, but had found her a little too earnest. She'd much preferred Carlota's company, Carlota being of a similar age and temperament to Beth. The two young women had delighted in ganging up on Xavi and teasing him mercilessly, teasing he'd always taken in the spirit it was given. The two women had kept in touch over the years, meeting up if Carlota was in Spain when Beth visited her grandfather and when Carlota visited England. By unspoken agreement, Carlota's bastard brother was never mentioned.

'She moved to Brussels a few months ago but uses home as her base whenever she's in the country.'

There was a tap on the dining room door, and then Salma came in with a tray of coffee, followed by three men and two women in suits: lawyers who most definitely did not concern themselves with human rights.

Their presence allowed Beth to compose herself properly, push aside all the memories assaulting her and shake off the tendrils of tension the mention of Salamanca had unfurled between her and Xavi.

Getting to her feet, she shook the lawyers' hands then positioned herself at the table facing Xavi, figuring she'd rather have him in her eye line than sit beside him and suffer his nearness.

It was a decision she soon regretted. The lawyers had given her folios and a heap of paperwork on the workings of the Rosbel Group so she could refamiliarise herself with it all, but instead of diving into the shareholder information, her eyes kept seeking Xavi.

The more she looked at him, the more her pulses kept racing into a canter and the more she was forced to concede just how well his longer, floppier haircut and trim beard suited him. How much sexier they made him, giving him an almost piratical edge.

Really, she should be glad she still found him so sexy, as it would make it easier to play the game of marriage until she took everything from him. Beth had tried to fake desire a few times in the years without him, but it had always ended in such a hopeless mess, she'd lost the will to even try.

He ended the call he was on and smiled triumphantly. 'Two weeks on Saturday.'

Sixteen days? She came within a whisker of gulping. 'At the Almudena?'

His triumph grew. 'I told you they would fit us in.'

'Fit *you* in,' she commented drily. Her throat felt as dry as her tone. Plans for a wedding that twenty-four hours ago hadn't even been a thing were suddenly steamrolling ahead. Beth had suggested the Almudena Cathedral on a whim, an impossible challenge for Xavi to fail at, never expecting they'd be able to fit them in on such short notice.

She'd forgotten the sheer clout Xavi held in Spanish society, a clout that could only have grown in their eight years apart.

'You will courier your birth certificate and the other documents we spoke of?' one of the lawyers asked.

She smiled brightly. 'It will be my top priority.'

One of the lawyers who'd disappeared into Xavi's office returned with an armful of documents.

Soon, everything that needed to be signed was signed, hands were shaken and the small army of lawyers bustled out. Beth had politely declined the offer of lunch with the excuse—a truthful one this time—of having a plane to catch.

'I'll drive you to the airport,' Xavi said once she'd arranged for Salma to stay on and care for Diego until they returned from their honeymoon.

'I'm sure you must need to get to work, so don't worry about that. I can get a taxi.'

'I insist.'

She managed not to clench her jaw. She'd be marrying him in sixteen days. She needed to learn how to cope with being alone with him. 'Thank you.'

The summer sun was high in the late-morning air when they stepped outside. Protecting her eyes with her shades, Beth strode to the convertible car that had to cost more than her grandparents' house.

It was incredible to believe that soon she would have the money to buy her grandparents and her father a swanky new home each and make the equivalent dent in her bank account as buying herself a new jumper currently made in it.

'Still don't like being driven around?' she asked lightly once she'd strapped herself in and Xavi had lowered the roof, something for which she was grateful as it meant she didn't have to breathe in such heavy doses of his gorgeous scent. His scent was something else she hated him for. Why couldn't he smell like a sewer?

He put his shades on and grinned. 'No, I still don't like being driven around, but the relentlessness of my schedule means I'm reliant on my driver more than I would wish to be.'

'The downside of being the boss?'

'The perks make up for it.'

'And what are the perks?'

'Not being answerable to anyone.' He pulled out and joined the crawling traffic. 'As we're talking of jobs, what do you intend to do about yours?'

'I'll have to resign. It's too hands-on for remote working, plus it would be weird to stay when I'm going to be a major shareholder of the Rosbel Group. We consider loads of your brands to be our rivals.'

'*Our* brands,' he corrected, flashing a quick grin at her. 'Miss Amore is now *our* rival.'

'Another thing for me to get my head around.' She shook her overloaded head.

'Are you still a fashion buyer there?'

'I am indeed.' It was a job she loved and one she was damned good at.

'I imagine you're excellent in the role. As I remember, you were always more animated about the fashion side of the business than the corporate side.'

He was referring to the three months she'd spent shadowing Xavi and their grandfathers within the Rosbel Group before she'd had that final spectacular fallout with her grandfather.

He wasn't wrong. She'd found the whole process of turning the designs created into finished products fascinating, from identifying the next big fashion trend to sourcing the materials and accessories and getting the best price for them. Her vague life plan to do a degree in English Literature and then find a career she could use it for had bitten the dust. Beth had found her path.

'I considered training to be a designer, but then I remembered that I can't draw for toffee.'

He laughed. It was the deep, spontaneous sound she used to love, but now landed like nails on a chalkboard.

'I take it you didn't consider using your connections for a similar role within the Rosbel Group?'

'You know I didn't want to work for my grandfather.' He'd been insufferable to work for, a control freak who wouldn't have looked out of place in a spy movie cast as the baddie set on world domination.

She'd never grown to love him like she did her other grandparents, but they'd developed their own unique way of handling each other and making the grandfather-granddaughter relationship work. To Beth's mind, that had only been possible through her steadfast refusal to ever work for him again.

However much she'd not wanted to work for her grandfather was nothing to how she'd felt about Xavi. She'd rather have eaten worms than work, however indirectly, for him. The fashion world, though, had found its way into her blood, and she'd been grateful for it. She'd used the knowledge she'd gained from her grandfather and Xavi to blag herself an internship at a growing hip fashion chain based in Manchester and never looked back. Her job—the work itself and the fun, creative people who worked there—had saved her, had made her see she could live a happy and fulfilling life without Xavi de la Rosa.

When she'd taken her revenge and her marriage was over, she'd buy Miss Amore, she decided, and give everyone a pay raise.

She felt Xavi's gaze glance her. 'He never stopped hoping you would change your mind and join us.'

She smiled sadly. 'I know, but it was for the best that I didn't. We clashed too much to work together.'

'I remember.' A smile resounded in his voice as the traffic came to a stop. 'At times, it was like dealing with two rutting bulls.'

About to make a quip back at him, Beth's tongue

froze, her senses soaring to high alert a beat before Xavi slid a hand onto her thigh and gently squeezed. 'You cannot know how good it feels to have you back in my life.'

There was no time to react to his touch or his words as the traffic started moving again and Xavi moved his hand to put the car back in gear.

She blew out the breath she'd sucked in and tried to relax.

Theirs had always been an affectionate and physical relationship, and the kiss she'd instigated in the study had led him to believe that it was a side of their relationship she was willing—keen even—to resume. And she *was* keen, but only insofar that she would be using it as a weapon to destroy him with. His affectionately delivered words just then meant nothing to her, not after all his lies, but if she could resurrect even a fraction of Xavi's old feelings for her, it would make his fall when she pulled the rug out from under him taste that much sweeter. And the way to Xavi's heart was through his cock. If she kept him happy in the bedroom, he'd have no reason to believe she was plotting his downfall behind his back.

But she wanted to be in control of it. Fully, completely, entirely in control, and that one squeeze of her thigh had proved how easy it would be for her to lose it. It was disconcerting how quickly her senses had retuned themselves to his frequency to the extent her body had anticipated his touch before her mind had. She'd only been back in his orbit for a day!

'What about you?' he asked.

She hated that his voice still acted like nectar to her ears. 'What about me?'

'How do you feel about having me back in your life?'

'I don't know.' That, at least, contained a nugget of truth. Beth had been racked with such a tumult of emotions since her return to Spain that to narrow it all into one concise sentence was impossible. 'I'm still trying to wrap my head around everything.'

'You must feel something for me to have agreed to my proposal.'

With this, she was able to look at him, and with complete truthfulness say, 'Xavi, my feelings for you are as strong as they have ever been.'

'Good strong or bad strong?'

Time had dimmed how perceptive he could be.

She laughed and looked out at the other vehicles fighting the same fight through the traffic as they were. 'Let's just leave it at strong, okay?'

Although she wasn't looking at him, she felt his smile before she heard it in his voice. 'Strong feelings I can work with. Indifference would be a different matter.'

She wondered if he'd feel so positive about her strong feelings for him if those strong feelings manifested in her throwing vases at his head.

If only she did feel indifference for him. She might have been able to move on in her personal life. 'Indifference is one thing I don't think I could ever feel for you.'

'Good... Music?'

'Sure.'

Using voice commands, he selected an album of the

rock band he'd flown her to Germany to watch perform live.

Glad she had her sunglasses on, Beth closed her eyes and worked at not letting her inner feelings show on her face.

Mercifully, the traffic thinned out, and soon they were out of the city itself and homing in on the airport. Only the blasted music of the band she'd spent eight years avoiding listening to stopped her chest from lightening with relief, and when he pulled up at the express drop-off point, it took everything she had not to throw herself out of the car. It took even more to face him.

He was already looking at her, his shades removed. Wordlessly, he removed her sunglasses, too, and for a long moment simply gazed at her.

Bringing his face close to hers, he gently stroked her cheek. 'I know you still have doubts about me,' he said quietly, 'but I promise you will not regret your decision.'

The surge of emotion that rose so powerfully in her almost shocked Beth into silence. That Xavi could still read her so well despite all her efforts to conceal her true feelings was almost as frightening as the longing to believe him and the depth of her need to cover his hand and press it tighter to her cheek.

Gazing into eyes that were like melted dark chocolate, she whispered, 'Aren't you worried that you might regret it, too?'

His gaze didn't so much as flicker as he brought his face closer to hers. 'No, I'm not.'

Her lips were tingling with anticipation before she felt his breath on her lips and the tickle of his beard, and then she was filled with the glorious sensation of his tender caress on her lips.

He drew back with the ghost of a smile. 'You should go.'

Wishing she wasn't already craving more of his mouth on hers, she nodded.

He clasped the back of her head and nuzzled his nose to hers. 'Let me know when you've landed?'

Unable to resist, she pressed her mouth to his for one last kiss and murmured, 'I promise.'

When Beth strode into the airport on legs that felt all wobbly, she didn't have to look back to know he was watching her.

When Beth was out of his sight, Xavi turned the engine back on and drove away, resisting the temptation to abandon his car and follow her back to England.

He'd long wondered what her apartment, or *flat*, as she referred to it on social media, looked like. All she'd revealed were snippets; nothing that would allow a follower to identify the location or make an educated guess to it.

Her job, though, he knew a lot about, not just because of what she'd told him the few times they'd seen each other over the years or through what she'd posted, but because he owned the company.

Miss Amore was the first fashion chain he'd bought as a personal investment. He hadn't put it under the Rosbel Group umbrella, and only expert journalistic levels of digging would find his name as the owner.

He'd bought it on a Beth-like whim when she'd posted about starting an internship there. He'd experienced a lot of guilt in those days. Beth had only been expected to spend the summer in Madrid. It was because of Xavi that she'd given up her place at university to stay past the summer, and so when he'd learned that she'd decided to join the fashion world after all, he'd felt he owed it to her to smooth her path into it. It had been at his behind-the-scenes insistence that her internship had become a full-time position. Everything else she'd achieved had been through her own hard work.

She'd excelled without him. Thrived without him, personally and professionally.

Whereas he...

Xavi didn't like to remember the days when he'd had to bury himself in work just to get through the days without her.

CHAPTER FOUR

THE AIRPORT WAS BUSY, but Beth got through security with minimal queuing. After buying a coffee, she found herself a spot at the departure gate near a large, rowdy stag party. She knew it would be more prudent to wait until she was home before making this call, but with Xavi's kisses still fresh on her lips, she was fired up, almost buzzing with the desperate need to purge the tempest of emotion coursing through her. With her fellow travellers giving the stag party a wide berth, no one would be close enough to hear her side of the conversation.

She dialled the number, put the phone to one ear and a finger to the other to drown out the background noise.

A male American voice answered. 'Paul Haldron.'

'Hi, Paul, it's Beth Granger.'

A beat of silence.

'Do you know who I am?'

'I'm familiar with the name.'

'I'm Raul Belmonte's granddaughter.'

Another beat of silence.

'I'm his sole heir. Once probate's dealt with, I'll be the joint majority shareholder of the Rosbel Group.'

'I did wonder if that would be the case,' he said slowly. 'What can I do for you, Miss Granger?'

'Call me Beth, and it's not so much what you can do for me but what I can do for you. I understand you spearheaded the recent attempt at a hostile takeover.'

More silence and then a cautious, 'That's in the past. Xavi de la Rosa fought it and won.'

'He won because he had my grandfather's shares in his pocket. Those shares now belong to me...well, they will once probate's been granted. In a matter of months, they will be mine to do as I please, as will the rest of his estate, which I'm sure you must know is worth a *lot* of money.'

'Okay...?'

'How amenable would you be to selling your shares to me?'

He laughed.

'Paul...may I call you Paul?'

He laughed again. 'Sure.'

'Paul, Xavi will never relinquish his control of the Rosbel Group. You can try again, as many times as you like, but you won't win. He will never let you win.' And neither would she. The Rosbel Group belonged to the de la Rosas and Belmontes. She might not have her grandfather's name, but she was the only Belmonte left. Her grandfather and Ferdinand had built the company from nothing, and, having forced herself to think about it with rationality rather than emotion, she knew she couldn't destroy their legacy and put it in the hands of strangers. The only thing she wanted to destroy was Xavi.

'Cut to the chase, Miss Granger.'

'Beth,' she corrected. 'You can't beat him, but I can. Name your price.'

'I beg your pardon?'

'Your shares. I want them, and I'm prepared to pay any price for them.'

The silence this time went on for so long that she thought he'd hung up on her.

'You're preparing your own takeover?'

She ignored the question. 'You bought the shares as an investment fourteen years ago. Your investment has increased twelvefold. I'm prepared to pay more than the market price for them—I'm prepared to pay *any* price. You're a businessman, Paul. You invested in the Rosbel Group to make money. Now's the time to recoup that investment and make some serious money. Name your price.'

'I'll need to speak to my business partners,' he said slowly.

Beth smiled. Fired up with hurt and pain after her 2 a.m. call with Xavi, she'd thrown herself into researching Paul Haldron. His efforts to take over the Rosbel Group had cost him financially, and his other investments were performing poorly. He couldn't mount another hostile takeover attempt even if he wanted to. 'You do that. Get back to me with a price—I trust you will approach this with discretion?'

'Mom's the word.'

'Good, because for this to happen, not a word about it can leak.'

'Understood.'

The call over, she blew out a long breath. The buzz

that had taken her through that phone call—she'd channelled one of her favourite on-screen kick-ass female characters to get through it—was already plummeting, and she fought valiantly to recapture it.

Paul was interested, of that she was certain.

The first step towards Xavi's destruction had been taken.

Four days later, Beth read Xavi's message that had just pinged into her phone:

No budget. I'm in Paris and extremely busy. Please direct all messages during working hours that concern the wedding to Fenella. I will call you this evening when I've finished working to catch up. X

Her mouth tightened at his brush-off. The working day was done already. All she'd asked was the budget for her wedding dress.

She looked at all the boxes piled in her living room. Xavi had sent a team over to assist in packing up her life. If she wanted, she could fly back to Madrid right now. Her boss had taken her resignation well—too well, really. Beth had half expected pleas for her to change her mind, but *nada*. As soon as she'd told him the date for the wedding, he'd told her not to worry about working her full contracted notice. She had the feeling he'd have let her leave without working any of it, which was odd considering they didn't have an obvious candidate to take her role. He probably didn't want to miss out on his wedding invitation. She'd invited everyone she worked with. Let them enjoy the wedding of the century. After all, Xavi was paying for it all.

Oh yes, Xavi was paying for *everything*, and he was not holding back in the lavishing of his money. It was only his time he refused to lavish. He'd got her agreement to marry him, and now he was laying his marker and making sure to emphasise that their marriage would be nothing like their relationship of old. The kiss at the end of his message had been a sop, a marker of intent that quelled much of the guilt that kept nibbling at her.

She was reading the message a third time when her phone rang in her hand.

'Hey, Beth, Paul Haldron. I have good news for you.'

His next few words were lost in the sensation of white light flickering behind her eyes.

Forcing a long breath from her lungs, she casually said, 'And the price you require?'

It was as outrageous and greedy as she'd anticipated, but she was in no mood to barter. She wanted this done. 'Deal.'

'I did wonder if the news about your marriage would mean a change of heart.'

So news of their marriage had reached America. Xavi had put out a press release the day before. Any moment and the press would discover her location and descend on her. Anticipating this, Xavi had already sent a team of ex-special forces to keep watch over her and keep her safe.

Her answer was a clipped, 'Not at all.'

He gave a low chuckle. 'Lady, you must *really* hate him to be playing him for such a sucker.'

'My reasons are none of your business,' she informed him coldly. 'I'll be in England for another week or so, and I want an agreement in principle before I return to Madrid for my wedding. I imagine I'll be in a position to complete the purchase within three months, and I want things arranged so the moment I give the go-ahead, the transfer is made immediately.'

His laughter had a touch of patronising indulgence to it. 'Do you know how the transfer of shares works, lady?'

'I'm learning, but I do know how the power of money works, and if you want any of mine, you'll keep your mouth shut about this conversation—if Xavi hears even a whisper of our plans before the transfer takes place, the deal will be off and your march to bankruptcy will carry on at the pace it's currently travelling.'

She ended the conversation without saying goodbye.

Her heart was racing manically.

The ball was now well and truly rolling. Very soon, she would roll it some more to hoover up enough of the smaller shares to make her the majority shareholder of the Rosbel Group.

She had another read of Xavi's message and willed her heart to harden. Any feelings he held for her were secondary to his devotion to the business. He would dump her again in a heartbeat if he felt their relationship threatened his control of it in any way. She must never forget that.

Two weeks after she'd returned to England to pack up her life, Beth stepped out of Xavi's private plane and strode through late-afternoon air so thick with heat it shimmered.

The driver and passenger of the familiar black SUV waiting for her both got out before she reached them. The former started loading all her suitcases into the boot. The latter, in faded jeans, brown boots and a snug white T-shirt that emphasised the muscularity of his impossibly tall, wiry physique, simply gazed at her from behind his shades.

Making no attempt to kiss or embrace her, his firm lips curved into a lazy smile. '*Hola, mi vida*. Good flight?'

Just to hear his voice was to make her heart, racing with anticipation at seeing him again from the moment she'd woken, thump harder.

The longer she'd spent away from him, the more fully he'd invaded her mind. The wonderful memories of their six months together had fought with the awful memories of their sudden break-up and its aftermath, her resolve at what she was planning for him wrestling with guilt and doubt. So exhausted had the constant thoughts and heightened emotions left her that she'd kept falling asleep hours earlier than she normally would, only for vivid dreams to keep springing her awake.

The dreams had all centred around him. The worst one had been just last night when she'd dreamed of walking into his old bedroom while he was sleeping. Ellen had sat up beside him, naked just as she'd been in those vile nude pics she'd sent him all those years ago, smiling triumphantly at her, and Beth had realised it wasn't Xavi's bedroom but Ellen's bedroom, not their bed he slept naked in but Ellen's bed. And then Ellen had morphed into the woman from the New Year's party.

It had been her own whimpers that had pulled her awake from that one. Her chest had been icy cold ever since. If she could have delayed her return again, she would have done.

There would be no more delays. Xavi's mother was throwing a pre-wedding dinner party for a select number of family and friends that evening. As much as Beth would have preferred to stay away from Madrid until the wedding itself, she couldn't do that to Mireia. Xavi's mother had shown her nothing but love and had sent her the most wonderful message saying how delighted she was at the news that, finally, Beth would be marrying into her family.

However cold she felt inside, she wouldn't let Xavi see it. Beth's pride had dragged her out of bed in the early days of their break-up, had made her smile widely and embrace him the few times she'd seen him over the years and had made her pull herself together every time her heart stopped when he liked one of her posts or left a comment.

If not for her pride, she would never have recovered from any of it and if she was going to get through the next however long of marriage to him, she would have to cling to it tightly because the one thing she would never allow herself to do would be to fall apart in front of him. She would never give him the power to break her again. In the future, she would be the one with the power to break *him*.

Producing an easy-going smile, she said, 'I'd forgotten how convenient flying private is over economy.' The entertainment on her flight to England from Madrid had come courtesy of the rowdy stag party. She imagined they were still fighting off their hangovers.

Beth had thought about the stag party a lot during her return flight on Xavi's private jet. Thought, too, about the corresponding hen party. If the hen was as happy to be marrying as the drunken stag who'd got to his feet approximately every ten minutes to yell out, 'I'm getting *married*!' for all the plane to hear, then she thought they would have a good chance of making their marriage work.

Eight years ago, Beth would have been the happiest hen in the world.

His lips curved. 'More leg room, too.'

'How would you know? You consider first class to be slumming it,' she teased. Xavi's first holiday had been to his family's private Caribbean island when he'd been three months old, every whim catered to by a fleet of staff. Beth's first holiday had been to a decrepit British holiday resort when she'd been six as part of a newspaper cut-price deal. Her bed had been little bigger than a cot, which had been better than what her poor grandparents had had to deal with—the moment they'd climbed into their bed, it had collapsed beneath them. It had rained the whole week, too.

The curved lips widened into a grin. 'Can I help that I've been raised to have rarified tastes?'

'You've been spoiled your whole life.'

He laughed and swept an arm to the car. 'Come on, let's get you to your new home.'

* * *

The car's cabin was wonderfully cool, a relief after that short blast of Spanish heat that had warmed even her ice-cold chest a little. At least, Beth told herself, it was the heat that had warmed it, not being back in Xavi's orbit. If only the years had lessened his sex appeal by even an iota instead of enhancing it.

'Are your family and friends ready for tomorrow?' he asked once the car started moving.

Breathing through her mouth to stop the potency of Xavi's scent doing too much damage to her senses, she nestled against the door and twisted around so she was facing him. First thing in the morning, the eight members of her English family, her five closest friends and fifteen of her colleagues were being collected from their homes to be driven to their closest airports, then flying first class to Madrid and being put up in Madrid's finest hotel, all expenses paid, courtesy of Xavi. 'Yes. Everyone's very excited, especially my dad and my nan. Fenella and the rest of your staff have done a fabulous job getting it all arranged, so thank you for that.'

'They were happy to do it.'

She kicked her heels off and casually asked, 'How's everything going with my grandfather's estate?'

They'd spoken every evening in her absence, but they'd been short conversations. Xavi had been far too busy getting his affairs in order to take time off for their wedding and five-day honeymoon to hold a conversation that involved more than checking in with her. She hadn't needed to pester him to know his crack team of lawyers would be pulling out all the stops to get probate done swiftly. After all, it was in Xavi's interest for it to be completed as speedily as possible.

'The grant of probate should be ready within the next couple of weeks.'

'That soon?' She'd assumed it would take a few months at the least, even factoring in Xavi's diligence.

'Your grandfather was a meticulous man who left his affairs in exemplary order.'

That he had been, although *control freak* probably described him better. Domestically, he'd been fastidious about everything, from the correct way to hang a towel to demanding Beth straighten the cushions when getting up from a sofa. He'd been far worse within the workplace.

By the time he'd died, Beth had become so used to the control-freakery that she barely noticed it, let alone let herself get riled up about it. It was just the way he was, and she liked to think that if her mother had lived, she, too, would have learned to ignore the infuriating aspects of his nature... Or maybe not. Beth hadn't been raised by him or married to him. She'd only known him in his twilight years and then only sporadically. It wasn't just her mother who'd left him, but her grandmother, too.

As Beth had eventually learned from her father—her grandfather had adamantly refused to discuss the subject—Marta had been much younger than Raul. When she'd left him, she'd been so desperate to get away from him that she'd agreed to leave their only child with him. She'd taken the payoff and lived her life in quiet solitude, passing away ten years earlier. A part of Beth wished she'd known about her before she'd died so she could have tried to reach out to her, but another part was glad she hadn't. Beth's mother had given her life so Beth could live. Beth's grandmother had left her twelve-year-old daughter with the husband she despised. While Beth had suspicions as to why, she doubted she would ever know the truth. The dead couldn't speak. Beth was the only one of the bloodline still alive.

'That you are his only legitimate heir helps, too,' Xavi added, unwittingly tapping into her thoughts. 'There will be a hefty inheritance tax bill to be paid, but your grandfather made provisions for that. There is no reason to believe everything can't be signed over to you when we get back from our honeymoon.'

Her smile at this needed no practice. Whenever her conscience gnawed a little too deeply at the wheels she'd set in motion, all she had to do was bring up Ellen's time-stamped photo of Xavi asleep in her bed three days after he'd kicked Beth from his bed and remember his barefaced lie for resolve to steel her spine.

Their whole relationship had been a lie. Beth would have chosen to live the rest of her life in a grotty bedsit than live without Xavi. He'd not even given her the chance to make adjustments to their relationship so he could devote more of his time to the business, just off the bat dumped her like she was an unwanted plaster that needed ripping off his skin.

She *had* distracted him from his work, that had been true, but he'd let her. They'd had sex in his office more times than she could remember, and he'd been more than happy to go along with her impulsive, often madcap whims, whether that was deciding at three in the afternoon on a Friday to drive to Barcelona for a long weekend or gatecrashing a party because the music pumping from the house had been so enticing—that had been a brilliant night—or whisking him off to Ibiza with zero notice to visit its hippy market she'd just read about.

If he'd ever said no to her she would probably have pouted, but would have accepted it. If he'd said she had to confine her impulses to outside working hours or do them without him, she would have accepted that, too. Instead, he'd severed their relationship without discussion. Whether he'd always planned to bed Ellen or if Ellen had just been a perk of being single again, Beth didn't know nor care to know. It didn't make any difference. Ellen had just been a huge dose of salt rubbed into a wound that had never healed.

It would heal soon, though, when she took the Rosbel Group from him. With probate only weeks from being granted, she could be in a position to take it from him sooner than she'd hoped. She had an agreement in principle with Paul Haldron for the shares he controlled. Once they were in her name, she would own 45 per cent of the Rosbel Group. She was already sounding out wizards of the financial world to act on her behalf in hoovering up the smaller shares until she reached the magic 51 per cent for it.

Xavi was a barefaced liar who'd stolen her dreams and her future and broken her heart beyond repair, and now she was returning the favour.

There was nothing to feel guilty about.

CHAPTER FIVE

A SHORT WHILE LATER, and Beth had to work to maintain her smile when they drove through the wide, open arch of a stunning white-and-red Baroque building with turrets on its roof and came to a stop in an immaculate courtyard that edged sprawling lawns ringed with enormously high trees and a pond so big she wasn't sure if it shouldn't be called a lake.

It was exactly the kind of home she'd once dreamed of them living in, and she was glad she couldn't cry because knowing Xavi had gone ahead and bought their dream home without her filled her with emotions it was hard to breathe through.

Luckily, the time it took for him to whisk her to the top floor in a private elevator that needed his fingerprint to operate gave her time to compose herself.

Inside, the vastness of the high-ceilinged open spaces came as no surprise—Beth's months of living in Spanish opulence had inured her to what incredible wealth could buy you—but the tastefulness of it all did. Neutral walls were enlivened with an eclectic mix of artwork, the mass of dark leather seating richly inviting.

Hating to imagine Xavi consulting with a lover—

Ellen? Appendage lady?—over the interior, she stepped out onto the living room's balcony to breathe in the warm air, and soaked in the grounds from this new perspective.

It was hard not to sigh with wonder at it all, and just incredible to believe something like this existed in the heart of Madrid.

'This place must have cost you a fortune,' she commented when Xavi stood beside her at the balustrade.

'It's my most expensive piece of real estate, but worth every cent.' She felt his gaze turn to her. 'What do you think? Can you be happy here?'

She tightened her grip on the iron railing and fought her throat from closing.

Eight years ago, she would have been ecstatic. As amenable as the de la Rosas had been to her practically living with them, Beth had longed for her and Xavi to have a place of their own. As much as they'd spoken of buying a place just like this, she'd have been happy anywhere so long as it was with Xavi.

Eight years ago, she'd been a naive fool.

She brought a smile to her face and said, 'Waking up to this view every day will make me happy.'

The glass door opened, and his housekeeper stepped out carrying a tray of coffee for them.

Taking a seat at the balcony table, Beth tried not to wonder how many other women had taken this very seat.

'Is the whole top floor yours?' she asked once the coffee had been poured and they were alone again.

'The whole building is mine,' he said. 'I rent the other apartments out.'

'You bought the *whole building*?' If she were judging it by London standards, she would estimate it could be divided into homes for a minimum of ten families, all living in plentiful space and luxury. By Manchester standards, twenty families.

A muscular shoulder lifted. 'Why own a part of something when you can own the entire thing?'

'You do have a thing about owning the entirety of things, don't you?' At his raised eyebrows, she added, 'The primary reason you're marrying me is so you can keep control of the entirety of the Rosbel Group.'

His shaded stare stayed steady on her. 'Yes, keeping control of the company is my primary reason for marrying you, but that doesn't make my other reasons redundant, and it doesn't change that you're the only woman I've ever wanted to marry.'

Rather than throw her coffee over him, she laughed and fixed her gaze back on the distant lake-size pond. Figures she thought looked small enough to be children were paddling in it. If their child had lived, it could have been one of those children. It would have just turned seven, and it never failed to hurt her heart that it hadn't lived long enough for her to know its sex.

'I mean it, Beth. No one else has come close to you.'

'Gosh, I am *honoured*.' She would not give him the satisfaction of saying no one had come close to him, either...not that she believed him. Xavi would say whatever needed saying and do whatever needed doing until he had his ring on her finger.

'You don't believe me?'

She shrugged. 'Does it matter when we're getting married in two days?'

'It matters to me.'

'Regaining my trust in you is going to take time.' Until the end of days and then some.

An edge came into his voice. 'If you don't trust me, why agree to marry me?'

So I can destroy you.

'Because you made such a convincing pitch for it?' She laughed again and shook her head, wondering why she couldn't just outright lie to him. 'Xavi, let's not pretend that everything's going to be chocolate sprinkles straight away. We need to get to know each other again.' She removed her sunglasses to look more directly at him. 'Just remember, if I didn't hold such strong feelings for you, I would never have agreed to marry you. I'm uprooting myself from my life, all of it. Everything I've built for myself these last eight years. I'm leaving my family and friends behind and walking away from the job I love for you.'

Removing his shades, too, Xavi studied Beth with the same intensity he'd studied her at her grandfather's wake.

Beth had warned him that she'd changed from the young woman he'd been in love with all those years ago, but he'd already known that before proposing. He wouldn't have contemplated taking this path if he'd thought they were the same people as they'd been eight years ago, but the changes to Beth weren't just in general maturity; there was something else, too, something that had been gnawing at his gut since she'd returned to England and had grown stronger with each excuse to delay her return to him.

The Beth he remembered had fed on emotion. This Beth fed on logic and rationality. The passionate fire and zest for life that burned so bright in her had muted, and he couldn't shake the feeling she was smothering it deliberately, just like he'd been unable to shake the voice nagging in his head that something else was going on with her.

He pulled in a deep breath through his nose and reminded himself that she was here and that in two days she would be his wife. After eight years apart, he couldn't expect things to be *chocolate sprinkles* immediately—he needed to find some patience, a trait he was forced to admit was not on his list of attributes. Beth was right that he was spoiled, and being spoiled with women counted in that, too. Xavi had grown used to women pretending that the sun shone out of his backside and could see how easy it was for men in his position to believe it actually did. Not every man of his position had a younger sister called Carlota primed to bring him back down to earth at every given opportunity.

Beth had never treated him as if the sun shone out of his backside. She'd treated him as if he *were* her sun, but his family's wealth and standing had meant nothing to her. She'd loved him for him, and that had been as intoxicating as the sex between them, and now she was back in his life, marrying him and entrusting her shares to him and so securing his position within the Rosbel Group. She'd entrusted her grandfather's estate into his care, too; trusted him with billions in the form of assets, cash and shares. She trusted him where it most mattered; that was the important thing.

The second most important thing was that Beth was the only woman he'd ever wanted to marry, the only woman he'd envisaged having children with. That had never changed, and there was nothing to make him think they couldn't make it work. They still shared a humour, and the spark was still there between them, too.

A lot of marriages survived with less than spark and humour. He didn't think his parents' marriage had been miserable, but he couldn't remember it being particularly happy, either. That hadn't stopped his mother's utter devastation at his father's death. She'd wandered the rooms of their home like a wraith for months, unable to settle, unable to concentrate, incapable of caring for her three grieving children.

'You need to step up now, Xavi,' his grandfather, grieving the loss of his only son, had told him privately the night his father had taken his final breath. 'It is time for you to become a man. Your mother and your sisters need you. *I* need you.'

And so he'd stepped up to the mark his grandfather had set for him and become the man his family needed. He'd channelled the grief that had threatened to choke him and taken control of the household, from directing the domestic staff to ensuring his sisters did their homework and that Carlota, then only nine, brushed her teeth. He'd held everything together until his mother came out of her fugue, and then devoted his time to the studies he'd neglected for the sake of his family. Knowing his grandfather's retirement plans had been put on ice, he'd worked hard and earned his place at Oxford on merit, and completed back-to-back degrees. His studies done, he'd joined the Rosbel Group, ready, willing and able to be groomed into taking over from the two aging men who were both more than ready to devote their lives to their local golf course; and then within months, Beth Granger had appeared in his life, and for six months derailed him from everything that was important in his life.

Reaching across the small table, he took hold of her dainty hand and brought the tips of her fingers to his lips. 'I will make all your sacrifices worthwhile, I promise.'

Something flashed in her eyes before she leaned closer and clasped her fingers around his, her lips stretching into the upside-down heart he so loved. 'If I didn't know it would be worth it, I wouldn't be here.'

Their lips brushed together across the table. Closing his eyes, Xavi breathed her in. The heat from the sun enhanced the soft scent of her skin, which was a smell like nothing else on this earth. If its uniqueness could be captured, he'd get his perfumers to bottle it. They would make a fortune. But it couldn't be captured, and so it was a scent that belonged only to him, and in two days, Beth would belong only to him, too.

After pulling his mouth away, he gently tucked a lock of her English autumn-coloured hair behind one of her pixie ears. He'd longed to touch her since she'd stepped off the plane, but had resisted. Beth's kisses were just too potent for sensibility. He could still feel the effect of the kiss they'd shared in the study, had carried her taste on his tongue since she'd left to pack up her life in England. 'We need to get ready for my mother's dinner party.'

Those incredible crystal-clear eyes pulsed. 'Is this where we go to the bedroom?'

He kissed her again, a longer, deeper fusion. Rubbing his cheek to hers, he murmured, 'Patience, *mi vida*. We need to leave soon.'

Her hand clasped the back of his head, her lips parting, her tongue darting into his mouth to dance with his. 'You're going to make me wait?'

'You've made me wait for two weeks. Consider this payback.'

'I thought we were all mature now,' she teased seductively before sliding her tongue back into his mouth.

He returned the kiss... *Dios*, she tasted so damn good...and threaded his fingers deeper into her hair. 'Only until you kiss me, and then I am twenty-four again.' And when he was twenty-four, he'd been insatiable. The six months he'd spent with Beth had been the most hedonistic months of his life. He'd wanted her constantly.

He would not allow himself to fall back into that lust-blinded state again. This time, he would keep firm control of his libido and create clear demarcations between his work and his home, lines that had blurred beyond recognition when they'd first been together. Professionalism and propriety had gone out the window. Eight years on, and Xavi was still unable to look at the left side boardroom window without remembering how Beth had sat on its ledge with her skirt hitched up to her waist and her legs wrapped around him as he'd pounded into her. They'd barely straightened their clothes before his grandfather's executive assistant had strolled in with pastries for the imminent meeting.

Beth had stripped him of his self-control and professionalism, and the result had been the near destruction of everything. He'd spent years waking with cold sweats from dreams of his father shaking his head and sorrowfully saying, 'You promised to step up, Xavi.'

The first time that dream had struck him had been his first night in Milan after the meal where his grandfather and Raul had driven home how badly he'd taken his eye off the ball and screwed up. He'd woken in his hotel bed with a chest like ice and his skin clammy cold, and known there was no alternative. He had to end things with Beth.

When Xavi threw himself into something, it took all his attention. His feelings for Beth had consumed him and stolen his attention from the business and imperilled it. If he wanted to fulfil the destiny fate had set for him and step into the legacy his father had never been able to fulfil, it would have to be without her.

'If you were twenty-four again, you'd have screwed me in the back of the car on the drive here,' she said into his mouth. 'You didn't even try to kiss me.'

'That was deliberate. You, *mi vida*, are irresistible. One kiss is never enough. I didn't want our first screw in eight years to be a quickie in the car...'

'You screwed me nearly as many times in a car as you did in a bed.'

'That was then.' And he would never be that man

again. The intervening years had taught Xavi the needed art of separation. 'When we make love again, we're going to do it properly. When I take you, you will be naked in my bed.'

'I can get naked now, if you want?' she breathed.

Desire a heavy thrum in his veins, he groaned into her wet, hot, pliant mouth. *Dios*, he wanted to slide his hand beneath her plain cream top and cup the breasts that were anything but plain, lower his head and take a pale pink nipple into his mouth.

Her fingers dipped beneath the neck of his T-shirt. Her touch scorched his skin. 'Are you only kissing me now because there's a table between us?'

'Damned right.' Summoning all his control, he wrenched his mouth away and hauled himself to his feet.

One look at Beth's flushed cheeks was enough to make him suppress another groan. 'I'm going to take a cold shower in a guest room. Isabel will have unpacked your clothes by now—she will show you around our bedroom suite. Anything you need, she will provide it. We leave in an hour.'

Beth stood beneath the waterfall shower of the most stunning bathroom she'd ever been in and lathered herself with the gel Xavi's staff had unpacked for her, trying to breathe normally rather than just inhale tight, shallow snatches of air. Her heart was still thumping manically, her skin still so fevered it was hot to the touch. There was a pulsing ache between her legs she'd not felt in eight years. The closest had been two weeks ago in the de la Rosa study. Before that, she might as well have been dead from the waist down for all the sensation she'd felt there.

She wondered what Xavi would do if she were to seek out the guest room he'd hidden himself away in and stand before him naked. In their first incarnation, he'd never resisted an opportunity for sex. He'd been her slave for sex as much as she'd been his, but just as she was different from the Beth of old, he was different from the Xavi of old. She knew he still wanted her—she'd seen the hunger in his eyes and tasted his desire in his kisses—but in their first incarnation, he'd never hidden from it, had let his desires control him. The Xavi of today was a man who never relinquished control of himself.

Ellen's beautiful, spiteful face flashed into her vision. Ellen, who'd enjoyed Xavi's incredible lovemaking while Beth was still pregnant with his baby.

How many women had come after Ellen? Obviously, the appendage lady had, but how many others that she didn't know about? A handful? A baker's dozen? A score? Two score? More?

Beth had long ago learned not to torture herself with these nausea-inducing thoughts, but as she dried herself off, she refused to push them away. Tonight she would share Xavi's bed. They would have sex. Her heart would be at its most vulnerable. She needed to shield it. She needed to shield it through all the nights she would share his bed.

The bed they would be sharing was enormous and sinfully inviting. The bedroom itself, with its high ceiling, abundance of mirrors, seductive artwork and blue velvet soft furnishings, was sinfully inviting, and she forced herself to wonder how many other women had been invited into it. How many other women had made use of the shared dressing room? How many other women had sat at this dressing table and applied their makeup?

How many of those women had he lost control with?

By the time she was dressed, her hair dried and smoky eye makeup done, Beth's stomach churned so badly with self-inflicted nausea she doubted she'd be able to eat anything that evening.

Breathing as slowly and as deeply as she could, she took stock of her reflection.

When she came back to this room later that evening, she would enjoy Xavi's gorgeous body and let him enjoy hers. She would let him take her as many times as he wanted…and he always wanted more. As the weeks of their marriage passed, she would shamelessly use sex as her weapon of choice to break his defences and drive him wilder and wilder until she was buried as deeply in his head and heart as he was buried in hers, but through it all she would be full in control of herself with her heart shielded. The only control that would be broken would be Xavi's.

And then she would destroy him.

When Beth joined him with two minutes to spare in the living room, Xavi's heart doubled in size with just one beat.

Glass of whisky in hand, he got to his feet and drank in the stunning, colourful vision before him.

Wearing a floral sleeveless maxi dress that cinched

at the waist and emphasised her voluptuous feminine curves, its autumn colours perfectly complemented her long red hair, loose and gleaming under the last rays of the setting sun penetrating through the windows. The dark tan of her wedged sandals perfectly matched the handbag slung over her shoulder.

As confident in her skin as a catwalk model, she strode towards him with a wide smile. 'You look *good*!'

Before he could respond, her arms hooked around his neck, and he was engulfed in a cloud of freshly showered and perfumed Beth.

'This is where you tell me that I look beautiful,' she reminded him brightly, her face straining up to his for a kiss.

'You always look beautiful,' he assured her truthfully before pressing his mouth to hers. He allowed himself only the smallest taste before breaking the kiss and removing her hands from his neck. He took a step back and laughed at her pout. 'Later, *mi vida*.'

She tilted her head and pouted again, but her eyes were dancing with a knowing that made his veins thicken and loins tighten, and when the crystal glass was prised from his hand and she tipped the remaining liquid down her throat and wiped her mouth with the back of her hand with a flourish, he shook his head and laughed. *Dios*, Beth made even the stealing of his drink sexy.

Diving his fingers into her glorious hair, he gazed into her eyes. 'I take it back—you haven't changed at all. You're still fabulously crazy.' Crazy in the best way. He'd never suffered a moment of boredom with Beth.

Her lips formed their upside-down heart. 'Only to a degree. I've learned to control the crazy...to a point.'

He rubbed his nose to hers and inhaled her skin. 'Good. You wouldn't be you without it. Now, let's get out of here before we're forced to call the wedding off on account of my mother killing me for being late to her dinner party.'

'How many people are going to be there?' Beth asked as their driver navigated the busy early-evening Madrid streets filled with tourists and locals alike heading out for meals and drinks and whatever else people did when the working day was done.

Xavi rarely did anything when the working day was done, mainly because his working day was never done. The grandfathers had split the running of the Rosbel Group, Xavi's grandfather controlling the financial side, Raul controlling the creative side. Xavi controlled all of it, and with Beth's shares he could maintain that control until the day came that *he* chose to cede it. If fortune were in his favour, that control would be ceded to one or more of his and Beth's children.

'She said it was only close family and friends.'

'So half of Madrid, then?'

He met her eye and grinned. 'You know my mother.'

She smiled in agreement.

It seemed incredible to him that he could still read her smiles.

'Is Blanca going to be there?' she said. 'I meant to message Carlota earlier and ask.'

'She flew in a couple of hours before you landed.'

'How does she feel about us marrying?'

'I haven't spoken to her about it, but I don't imagine she has any negative thoughts. She always liked you.'

'I always liked her, too... Is she still very serious?'

'Blanca was born serious. I think our father's death solidified that aspect of her nature.'

Her smile turned into one of sympathy, and she slid her hand across the small but deliberate divide he'd created between them to squeeze his. 'Is she seeing anyone?'

'If she is, she hasn't mentioned it.'

'What about Carlota? Is she still seeing that archaeologist?'

'What archaeologist?'

She shook her head and chided, 'Do you actually know *anything* about your sisters?'

He tried not to feel defensive at a subtle rebuke similar to ones his mother often made. 'I know they're both getting on well in their careers. Their personal lives are none of my business unless they choose to make it my business.'

'If I had siblings, I'd make their business my business. I'd want to know everything about their lives.'

'Why?'

'I like knowing the minutiae of my friends' lives, so I imagine my nosiness would be even stronger with a sibling.'

Beth, Xavi remembered, had always wanted siblings. He'd often thought one of his attractions for her had been the female-dominant contingent of his household. She hadn't just loved him, she'd loved his mother and sisters, too, especially Carlota. Although Carlota never spoke of it, he knew they'd stayed in touch over the years. He'd been glad of it; another tenuous way of keeping Beth in the periphery of his life.

Sure enough, when they reached the villa and got out of the car, Carlota was straight out the front door to greet them. With a squeal that made his ears hurt, she bounded down the marble steps to throw her arms around Beth, an embrace that was enthusiastically returned.

Inside, the villa overflowed with people. One glance around the open-plan reception and Xavi figured every single aunt and uncle—his father had been an only child, but his mother was one of six—cousin and second cousin was there. Entertaining, he'd long ago realised, had been his mother's way of coping with the loss of her husband. Once she'd pulled herself out of the worst of her grief, she'd taken to throwing parties of all shapes and sizes for any given reason, and had the space and money to feed whole armies if she so wished. Tonight was her way of celebrating her eldest child marrying before the press turned the nuptials into a circus.

Soon, everyone piled around the tables in the garden to drink whatever the hell they pleased and feast on a variety of tapas before the chefs brought out pans of traditional paella.

One of the things Xavi had always so loved about Beth was her unashamed love of food. There was none of the nibbling at dishes the way his mother and sisters did or the few women he'd dated over the years did: She attacked it the way she did everything else in life, with gusto and relish. It was sexy. Watching her expertly peel the shell off a langoustine was sexy. Watching her screw up her expert shell peeling and splatter her cheek with paella juice and burst into laughter as she dabbed at it with a napkin was sexy, and it came to him, really came to him, that in two days he'd be marrying her. After eight years of emptiness, the time was finally right for them.

Seated directly opposite him, Beth's stare caught his. His heart caught in his throat.

She raised her glass of white wine to him.

He lifted his bottle of beer to her.

Carlota, seated to Beth's right in complete disregard of their mother's table plan, whispered something in her ear that made her laugh again and take a large drink of her wine, which she promptly spilt down her chin to even greater peals of laughter.

'I'm glad she's giving you a second chance,' Blanca said softly from the seat beside him.

His eyes still on Beth, he nodded. 'So am I.'

'You're a lucky man. Not many women would forgive what you did to her.'

His defensive hackles immediately rose. 'All I did was end a relationship that wasn't working for me, nothing that people haven't been doing since the dawn of humanity.'

'It was the way you ended it. You forget I was there. I saw her before you got home. It was the happiest and most excited I'd ever seen her, which is a high bar for Beth, and then I heard her pleas and her sobs. We all heard her, and we all saw the state she was in when she left. You broke her, Xavi.'

'That was a lifetime ago,' he dismissed. 'And I didn't break her. She was upset at the time, I don't deny that, but she got over it quickly. She understands why I ended it the way I did, and she agrees I was right to do so. Neither of us was ready for what we had then.'

'Sure about that, are you?'

'Yes,' he said, his tone brusque and with a hint of irritation enough to tell his sister he would listen to no more on the subject.

Beth's musical laughter cut through the tense air that had formed between Xavi and Blanca, and he shrugged off the irritation and strange discomfort his sister's unwanted probing had set off in him and focused his attention back on the woman about to retake her place as the most important person in his life.

In two days, this fabulously crazy, vivacious woman with a zest for life was finally going to be his wife. Tonight, though…

Tonight he would make her his again, and this time she would be his forever.

CHAPTER SIX

'You looked like you enjoyed yourself,' Xavi commented as they drove out of the de la Rosa estate.

'I had a great time.' Beth smiled wistfully. 'It was lovely seeing everyone—I'd forgotten how big your mother's side of the family is.' The first time Beth had seen the whole family together, she'd felt incredibly intimidated, a state of affairs that lasted only seconds as everyone had made her so welcome. She'd had no qualms about seeing them all again, and she left with a lovely warmth in her chest, which made a wonderful change from the ice that had been in it since she'd wrenched herself out of that horrible dream.

Her cheeks had received more kisses in one night than the whole of her face had received in eight years.

'It was a shame your grandfather couldn't be there,' she added. She'd managed only a few short words with Ferdinand at the funeral.

'He will be at the wedding.'

'Good.' She tried to sound like she meant it. She liked Ferdinand as much as she liked the rest of Xavi's family, and it had struck her that evening that they would all be there at the wedding, would all hear them exchange their vows and believe Beth meant hers. Guilt was already trying to scratch at her over this. When she took the Rosbel Group from Xavi, they would all wonder if she'd been playing them, too. She could only hope they all, Mireia, Carlota and Blanca especially, found it in their hearts to forgive her. None of the women cared about the business, not in the way Xavi did, and had no financial stake in it anymore, but she didn't want to hurt them. If she could stay married to the family without having to stay married to the man, then she'd take it in a heartbeat.

She had to stop thinking like this and keep her focus on her revenge. Her professional life had gone forward in leaps and bounds these past eight years, but her personal life had been stuck in stasis. She'd tried to move on, but it had proved impossible. Xavi had ruined her for every other man. Until she eradicated him from her life once and for all, she would never have the family she had once so craved. She wouldn't be capable.

They would already have a family if he hadn't put his precious business above his feelings for her. There was no way of knowing if their child would have survived if they'd stayed together, but Xavi would have been there for her through the loss, and they would surely have tried again.

Knowing from the tightening in her stomach and chest that she was on the cusp of falling into melancholy, she breached the deliberate distance he'd once again created between them and leaned into him. For her revenge to have maximum impact, she needed to keep focused.

'Are you nervous for Saturday?' she asked softly, resting her hand on his lap.

In the old days, he would have covered her hand and slid it up to his groin. This time, he covered it and squeezed. 'I don't do nerves, *mi vida*.'

And neither would she. Nor guilt.

Twisting her bottom, she draped her leg over his lap and tugged her hand out of his hold to press it to his chest.

He gripped the thigh lying on him, but made no effort to slide his hand up the skirt of her dress.

'What are you doing?' he asked with husky bemusement when she undid a shirt button and slipped her hand through the gap to place her palm on his naked skin. Her heart trembled at the familiar warmth of his smooth skin and the softness of the hair covering it, and then trembled more violently to feel the strength of his heart beating beneath it.

In their old life, Beth had spent hours with her head on his chest while he slept, listening to the rhythmic beat that kept him alive while he was unconscious. Death was something Beth had always had a strong respect for, a respect that verged on fear. As a child, she'd often woken in the night and slipped into her father and grandparents' bedrooms to check they were all still breathing. With her family, that check had been enough for her to go back to sleep. With Xavi, she'd woken regularly through the night, that switch in her brain pinging her awake just to check he hadn't slipped beyond the veil.

Every morning, without fail, she messaged her father

and grandmother with two words: Good morning. She never felt settled in her skin until she heard back from them, and now, with the weight of Xavi's heart thumping so strongly against the palm of her hand, she wondered for the first time if she'd become such a prolific social media poster because the likes and comments Xavi gave them were the proof her subconscious needed that his heart was still beating.

So frightening was this thought that instead of answering with something flirty and seductive as she'd intended, her whispered, 'I just need to touch you,' came from her trembling heart.

His grip on her thigh tightened.

By the time the driver had dropped them off and they were taking the elevator back up to the apartment, Beth had shaken off most of the strange thoughts that had almost caused her to reevaluate the meaning behind her social media content.

She'd never lied to herself about Xavi always being at the forefront of her thoughts whenever she pressed the post button, but that had always been because she knew he kept an eye out for her posts, and she wanted him to see what a fabulous life she was living without him. To think it had meant more than that…

Nope. Not possible. All she felt for Xavi was hate. In fact, she might just pluck some of his body hairs out while he slept and make a voodoo doll with them. Obviously, she'd need to do an internet search on DIY voodoo dolls, but she was creative and could follow instructions. It would be easy. She'd just have to learn where to poke the pins in so it only maimed him rather than anything serious, because if she...

There was a lurch in her stomach and heart that made her reflexively squeeze the warm fingers laced through hers.

'Are you okay?'

She met the concerned dark brown eyes and nodded.

His forehead furrowed. 'You've lost colour on your face. Are you sure you're okay?'

She forced another nod and, because she couldn't tell him the truth, said the first thing that popped into her head. 'Someone just walked on my grave, that's all.'

'Is that one of those English sayings?'

This time, she managed to dredge a smile with her nod. 'You know that sensation when a shiver runs through you with no warning or apparent reason? That's what the saying refers to.'

Right, so voodoo dolls were out. She might be working to destroy him, but she didn't want to *hurt* him.

She didn't just not want to hurt him, she *couldn't* hurt him. Her brain wouldn't even let her think of it, not even as a macabre joke.

The elevator door opened. Instead of stepping out, Xavi cupped her cheek and brought his face down to hers and murmured, 'Very soon, *mi vida*, the only shivers you will experience will be the shivers of pleasure.'

Just to feel his breath on her face was to send shivers of sensation racing through her and remind her that hate wasn't the only emotion she felt for him. It wasn't even the strongest.

There was the lightest touch of his mouth to hers before his eyes gleamed, and he turned to lead her into the apartment.

Her heart beating erratically, Beth kept her hand in his firm grip and concentrated on breathing as they walked closer and closer to the bedroom.

It had been many years since Xavi had sat propped against a headboard in a bed with such heavy anticipation coiling through his veins and with the beats of his heart feeling so weighty. Even his skin felt like it had come to life; electrical tingles charging through his atoms.

He'd finished in his section of the bathroom first. He'd showered, heavily aware of Beth showering on the other side of the divide. There was no door separating them, just the marble wall that divided his side from hers. If he'd wanted to, he could have walked around the end of the divide and joined her.

The Xavi of old would have knocked the wall down to join her if it had saved seconds walking.

He wasn't that Xavi anymore. He was no longer driven by his desire for Beth. He controlled his desire, not the other way round. He would have taken her without thinking in the study that day of the funeral, but only because he'd not been prepared for her 'chemistry test.'

He was prepared now. Prepared for the rest of his life. He could delay his gratification as he'd proved numerous times that day. Showering with a full-on erection just to imagine Beth lathering herself naked only feet from him was but one of the many tests to his control. He could have taken her in the car on the way from the airport and the drive to and from his family villa. He could have taken her before they'd left for the dinner. He could have taken a casual walk to the hidden spot at the bottom of the de la Rosa garden and taken her there as he'd done a dozen times before.

He'd never had to think about delaying gratification in the intervening years. His control had never come close to being compromised...well, except in those early days after he'd ended things with her, but that had been a different form of control he'd struggled to keep hold of.

The bathroom door opened.

Even before she emerged into the dimly lit room, his arousal throbbed and hardened into rock.

His chest filled, and his throat ran dry.

He'd expected her to emerge naked. Instead, she wore a skimpy translucent black negligee that both covered and revealed her most intimate, feminine parts and showcased the spectacular curves that had always driven him so wild.

Long hair loose around her shoulders, full, weighty breasts gently swaying, she stepped slowly to him.

He swallowed for breath as he took in the wide hips and shapely legs, the softly rounded belly that cinched in at the waist, the slender arms...

She reached the foot of the bed and stopped.

Crystal-clear green eyes locked on his, she pinched the hem of the negligee with both hands and slowly hitched it up, past the juncture of her thighs and the soft, trimmed red bush he'd once shaved until they decided they both preferred it in its natural form. Higher it rose, over her navel, her breasts and pale pink nipples rising and stretching as she lifted it over them, and then it was travelling the length of her slender throat and briefly over her face before it was dropped onto the floor and the hair captured in it was tumbling back down and Beth was staring at him with such naked desire it was all he could do not to launch himself at her, throw her onto the bed and plunge deep inside her.

She climbed onto the bed and crawled towards him like a lioness hunting her prey.

Beth's heart was hammering so hard and fast it had become an indistinct burr. The bedroom's dim, romantic lighting perfectly accentuated the piratical darkness of Xavi's features and turned his body into light and shade. The only movement of his features and body was the flaring of his nostrils and the pulsing of his hooded eyes.

She fought for breath as she took in the changes time had made to his glorious body. So much was the same, but so much was different, too. He'd filled out more than his clothing had revealed, his wiry body far more muscular than it used to be. She didn't need to touch his washboard stomach to know it was harder than it had been when she'd been the most important person in his world, and she squashed the swell of misery that rose to wonder how many other women had already enjoyed this version of him.

She couldn't think about them. Mustn't. Not here in this bed. Not when the one thing that hadn't changed about him was standing proudly to attention, the tip practically touching his belly button.

Before Xavi, she'd always imagined she would find a real-life penis disgusting. Raised in a culture where pornography was rife and the boys of her school thought it hilarious to send dick pics to unwitting girls—a practice eventually stamped out by a determined headmistress and police liaison officers—she'd felt so violated and grossed-out at the unwanted pictures sent to her phone that she'd been in no rush to get intimate with anyone, certainly in no rush to see a male naked in the flesh.

That had all changed with Xavi. Oh, he'd been as horny as the male dogs in her school, but he'd been horny for *her*. He'd wanted Beth, not her vagina. She hadn't been the port in any storm to him. *She'd* been his port. He'd wanted to know *her*, all of her. He'd made her feel beautiful and sexy, and his delight in her body had banished any hang-ups she'd had about the size of her hips and backside. His penis, huge though it was, was something she'd learned to love and not fear. When they'd made love the first time, he'd taken such care of her that there had been hardly any discomfort, let alone pain.

She would have walked on burning coal laced with glass for him, and it killed her to know there was a tiny part of her that still would.

The texture of his skin was another thing that hadn't changed, and she trailed her fingers up his legs, marvelling and despairing that she remembered it so perfectly. Marvelled and despaired, too, that she was burning up to taste and touch him and to feel the exquisite joy of his possession.

He crooked a finger. Heat was blazing from the hooded eyes locked so tightly on hers. 'Come here,' he said thickly.

Suddenly furious with herself for letting her thoughts take control of her when she was on the first stage of her mission to take control of *him*, she ignored his beckoning finger and took hold of his cock.

'Beth…' His protest cut off when she closed her lips around it.

She could have cried. It even tasted of the same Xavi cleanliness as she remembered. It felt the same, too, a hard, almost glassy-smooth warmth on her tongue. She'd never been able to take it all in her mouth, but that had never mattered; she'd learned to drive him insane using her hands, too, even masturbating him between her breasts. She'd been shameless and wanton in her need to give him pleasure, and as she began to pleasure him now, his reactions fed the burn inside her, turning her on as effectively as if he'd been the one bestowing pleasure on her.

Fingers dove into her hair, his stomach brushing her forehead as he cradled her bobbing head with low groans until he gently lifted her face and gazed down at her.

Meeting his stare, her heart punched hard into her ribs, and the part of her that still loved him wanted to punch him as hard as she could for the way he was looking at her, as if she were his dream come to life and not the dream he'd only picked back up off the reject pile because she had something he wanted.

She was barely aware of being pushed onto her back until she was flat on the mattress and he was lying over her, still gazing at her in the way that made her heart sing and cry all at the same time.

Gently, he smoothed her fringe out of her eyes and then with her name a whisper on his tongue, he kissed her.

Although she'd spent so much of the evening aching to feel Xavi's lips back on hers, the crying part of her heart instinctively resisted his kiss. She wanted to make love to him, not the other way round. She wanted... *needed*...to control all of this, just as she'd controlled the intimacy that had brought them to this point.

His face lifted off her, his concerned stare locking back onto hers. 'What's wrong?'

To her utter horror, the tear ducts she'd spent eight years believing had run dry filled, the pressure that had been missing all these years burning the back of her eyes. The terror that they would spill out and he would see her cry and so see all the things she'd sworn to never let him see again was even stronger than the terror of losing herself in the pleasure of Xavi, and she speared the back of his head to pull his face back down to hers.

Their mouths fused, and in an instant she was close to being lost in the hunger of his kiss. Lips moving in a lusty, possessive dance, their tongues entwined, and Beth was helpless to do anything but cradle his head and drag her fingers through the soft, dark hair she'd once spent hours of her life stroking.

His weight lowered onto her, and then it wasn't just her mouth being crushed but her breasts and her stomach, sensation burning like a greedy flame through her as they became a tangle of entwined limbs.

'*Dios*, I have missed you,' he muttered into her mouth, words to make her want to cry and want to smash her fists into him, but then his lips dragged over her cheek and down her throat, and she fell back into her Xavi bliss.

The softness of his beard scraped her sensitised skin, a brand-new sensation that heightened the thrills, and when he took the hard peak of her breast in his mouth, her cries came from a place she had no control over.

Xavi had never considered himself a breast man until Beth had come into his life. He still didn't. It was *Beth's* breasts that turned him on so much, not just the weight and fullness of them but the way she writhed and moaned at his slavering worship of them. They were like marshmallow-filled pillows and tasted even sweeter, and he would gladly take his last breath suffocated in them.

He would gladly take his last breath anywhere so long as it was with her. Making love to Beth was like making love to a hedonistic heaven condensed into soft, womanly form.

He would never forget the first time they'd made love. He'd never known himself capable of exerting such control, and he would need similar control to draw strength from to stop himself falling back into the Beth spell that had once captured him so completely.

Breaking that spell had taken such focus and strength that he'd broken a part of himself in the process, a side effect of breaking her heart he'd always accepted.

All the years spent without her had been lived with the hazy thought far in the back of his mind that when the time was right, he would bring her back into his life.

That time was now, but this time, he would not allow her spell to capture the whole of him again.

Here and now, she was exactly where he wanted her, in his bed and in his arms, and he closed his mind of all thoughts and sank back into the heaven of Beth.

He kissed and licked every glorious inch of her flesh, sinking his fingers into the buttery soft skin, letting her cries and moans soak into his senses and feed his arousal. When he buried his face between her legs, he found her swollen and ready and radiating the soft, musky scent of her desire, a scent and taste that had lost none of the potency of old and darted straight into his burning loins.

Time had dulled the potency of the effect of Xavi's lovemaking. It must have done because *this*... He'd barely opened her up to him and pressed his tongue to her throbbing nub before Beth was riding a climax she'd been barely aware of forming under the weight of sensation ravaging the entirety of her being, a climax she was still riding when he kissed his way back up to her mouth.

Throbbing with desperation for his possession, she cupped his face tightly as their mouths and tongues entwined and lifted her thighs to wrap her legs around him. She could hardly breathe for anticipation, could hear nothing over the roar of her heart and the groans coming from Xavi's throat.

His hand skimmed her belly and her pubis as he reached for the weighty arousal straining against the top of her thigh, and she adjusted herself as he took hold of himself to press the tip right in the place they both needed it.

He filled her with one deep thrust.

The pleasure was so intense that she cried into his mouth, cries repeated as he began to move. With kisses as deep as his penetration, he drove into her with his hips, gripping her thighs to push them farther back and shrinking the world so it contained only them.

Lost in the paradise of Xavi's possession, Beth closed her eyes and sank into the swell of sensation. She was no more ready for her climax than she'd been for her first, and when it came, she could no more stop it than she could stop her heart from beating. It rippled out of her like a crescendo from deep within her, wave upon wave of pulsating rapture. So powerful were the ripples that she was barely conscious of Xavi's fingers biting into her thighs or the fevered drive of his thrusts, his deepening groans a distant echo until he came into sharp focus with a roar as he bucked into her one last, violent time, catching the swell of her abating climax and driving her back into a state of bliss that carried her off into another dimension.

CHAPTER SEVEN

Xavi splashed cold water on his face and took stock of his reflection. He expelled a long breath of relief to find it was the usual face staring back at him. The sensation that something had changed within him had been a delusion born from incredible sex.

Dios, incredible hardly did it justice.

Patting himself dry, he took another moment to compose himself and let his heart rate settle. One last look in the mirror to double-check it really was his face reflecting at him, and then he strolled back into the bedroom.

Beth was propped against the headboard in almost the same pose he'd waited for her in earlier. The difference was that she'd covered herself in the bedsheets.

'Hello, lover,' she said softly. There was a gleam in her eye that was so unexpectedly familiar, his throat caught. It was a gleam that only appeared after making love.

Breathing through the tightness, he padded to the bed. She pulled the sheets off with deliberate seduction, exposing her breasts as she welcomed him back.

He'd climbed off her only minutes ago. He shouldn't

be feeling fresh twinges in loins that were still fizzing from the strength of his orgasm. Shouldn't be, but Beth wasn't a normal woman. She was a goddess, and her breasts were manna from heaven.

What the hell. He wasn't losing anything by allowing her to tempt him into taking the manna into his mouth. This was their bedroom, and what they did in it had no effect on his working life or his self-control.

She sighed with pleasure at his sucking of her breast, and arched her back. 'God, that feels good.'

'*You* feel good.' He licked around the peak before gently biting it. 'Give me a little time, *mi vida*. I'm not twenty-four anymore.'

Her grin was sinfully wicked. 'Define *a little time*.'

Laughter rose, and he trailed his tongue up her throat and kissed her with a growl before flopping onto his back beside her. Wriggling down, she curled into him with her cheek on his chest.

For the longest time, they just lay there, Xavi stroking her back, Beth's fingers making circular motions around his nipple.

'How many men have you been with since we broke up?' he asked casually. It was a question he'd wondered virtually every day they'd spent apart.

Her fingers stilled. 'Why do you want to know?'

'Curiosity.' All the nights he'd had to drive away images of Beth sharing her goddess body with a faceless man. The times she posted a photo of herself out drinking with men… Those nights had been the worst for him.

'Curiosity killed the cat.'

'Is that another English saying?'

'Yep. Let's just say I've spent the intervening years enjoying my life and leave it at that.'

Beth would rather boil her head than tell him the truth.

'What if I don't want to leave it at that?'

'Then tough. I don't want to know about all the women you've been with.' Bad enough torturing herself with guesses. Having it confirmed...

'There haven't been many.'

Feeling like she'd been punched, she sat up and tightly said, 'I just said I don't want to know. I had no claim over you, and you had no claim over me, and I don't ever want to hear about or know which women you've shared this bed with.'

He gave a half smile and cupped her cheek. 'Only you.'

She went to slap his hand away, but ended up clasping it tightly. *'Liar!'*

'Beth, this place was our dream home. I couldn't bring another woman here. It would have felt wrong.'

Oh, why was he saying such things? 'You expect me to believe that?'

'Why not?' His eyes didn't even flicker. 'We've always been honest with each other. I bought this place with you in mind.'

She could do nothing to stop her burst of cynical laughter. 'Sure you did.'

'I think I always knew we'd end up back together.'

'Well, *I* didn't, so it's just as well I've been too career-focused to let another man sweep me off my feet, isn't it? Fully off my feet, that is,' she hastened to add. She would never let him even guess at the truth, and she was angry with herself for letting her jealousy at his other women seep out. 'Otherwise, you'd have bought this place for nothing and your wish to keep control of the Rosbel Group would have been screwed.'

He grinned. 'When you put it like that, I consider myself a fortunate man.'

How she *hated* his grin. Hated that it made her pelvis melt. Hated that it made her mouth want to reciprocate into a wide smile of its own. 'So you should. Who knows what I'd do with the shares if I were already married? I might feel obliged to sell them to one of those sharks to stop my husband being jealous about our history.'

He lifted his head, his grin widening. 'You wouldn't do that.'

'Wouldn't I?'

He palmed the underside of her breast and stretched his thumb to her nipple. 'You've changed in some respects but not in the ways that really matter. You're not someone who would do anything she didn't want to do and you would *never* screw another person over.'

'Maybe you don't know me as well as you think.' Oh, *why* did she keep trying to give him these damned cryptic warnings?

Holding her waist, he sat up and bowed his head to take her nipple into his mouth. 'I don't care how many men you've been with since me,' he said between licks and sucks. 'I know you better and more intimately than anyone.'

Sensation was filling her again, the heat in her pelvis bubbling back to life, and when he trailed a hand down her side to her thigh, she let him gently coax it over his lap so she was straddling him.

This was what she'd wanted when she'd agreed to marry him. Sex. Lots of sex. Not pointless pillow talk that hurt her heart.

What she must not do was allow herself to believe his lies, even if her heart ached for his words to be true. Xavi hadn't bought this gorgeous baroque building with her in mind. He was just saying what he thought needed saying to protect his interests.

He moved his attention to her other breast. She clasped the back of his head and raised her bottom so she straddled his arousal.

He gazed up at her with glazed eyes. 'No one could ever compare to you, *mi vida*. No one.'

Blocking his words out, she sank down on him with a long moan of pleasure.

'Does this place have a swimming pool?' Beth asked. Despite making love twice, she was still wide-awake, too many thoughts crowding her head to allow sleep to snake its way into her. Too many thoughts she did *not* want to let loose.

'You want to go swimming, *now*?'

Her cheek on his chest, the beats of his heart a steady, comforting—too comforting—sound, he didn't see her wistful smile that he still knew her well enough to know that when she asked a question like that, it generally meant she wanted to do it right away, not at some future date.

'Yes.' She lifted her chin to gaze into his eyes, and seductively added, 'But I don't have a swimming costume to hand so it'll have to be skinny-dipping.'

He made a groan-like laugh and shook his head before flashing his perfect teeth at her. 'What the hell. Come on. Let me show you my swimming pool.'

Her nudity wrapped in her silk kimono, Beth happily let Xavi, who'd slung a pair of shorts on, lead her out of the bedroom to a flight of stairs at the end of the corridor.

She climbed them and stepped out into the heady scent of night-blooming jasmine and twilight heat. Enough of the city was asleep for the black sky above them to glitter with stars, a sight that had her gaping—she couldn't remember seeing a star in the Madrid night sky before.

And then she lowered her gaze and gaped even harder, taking a long moment to soak in all she was seeing. 'How on earth did you get permission to do this?'

This being the most gloriously spectacular roof terrace. Its perimeter aglow with soft night-lights, its central pièce de résistance was an enormous swimming pool with a gorgeous mosaiced bottom of dolphins at play. Around it, plentiful plush seating for sunbathing and dining alike, along with a Caribbean-themed bar and an outdoor cooking area.

It was the panoramic view, though, that really took her breath away. It felt like the city went on forever. The pond-lake at the rear glistened under the lights of the stars like a private oasis of tranquillity, the trees surrounding it dark shadows melting into the night.

Standing behind her, Xavi put his hands on her hips and brushed his lips against her neck. 'Money and power talk.'

Surprise and disappointment lashed her even as shivers of excitement coiled up her spine. 'Bribes?'

'No, *mi vida*.' His hands were working on the sash of her robe. 'There is no need for bribes when you pay for the restoration of many of your home city's historical monuments and fund numerous shelters and rehabilitation units.'

Relieved, although why she didn't know, supposed it was that she didn't want to think the Xavi of old who'd always taken pride in the Rosbel Group being built on honest endeavour could have changed *that* much, she closed her eyes and leaned back into his strength. 'You've become a philanthropist?' Philanthropy made much more sense.

'Don't sound too impressed—it is all for the sake of my soul. I'm following in the footsteps of my father and grandfather. They taught me that with great wealth comes great responsibility.' As he spoke, he cupped her breasts and squeezed them in the way she so liked. 'Also, Blanca is always keen to remind me of the biblical quote about it being easier for a camel to go through the eye of a needle than for a rich man to enter the kingdom of heaven, and on the off chance that she's right, I prefer not to take any chances.'

She laughed and wriggled her bottom provocatively against his arousal. 'And how much of her personal wealth has Blanca given away?'

Still squeezing a breast, he slipped his other hand

down her belly, bending her forward a little. 'At least half of it to various human rights charities. Carlota uses hers to fund the archaeological digs she goes on—her work benefits people in a very different way, but as she is always keen to tell Blanca, humans need to know where they come from and the journey that took us to where we are today.'

'To think they could both just sit on their backsides and live off their trust funds...mind you, that applies to you, too.' The de la Rosa family's fortune had been secured when Xavi's father was a child. Their vast portfolio, even outside the business, meant none of them or future generations ever needed to work.

Xavi could have married her eight years ago and spent his life doing exactly what he was doing to her now with barely a dent to his wealth.

'My father had such a strong work ethic that he would turn in his grave if we sat around doing nothing all day.'

'You've all got way too much energy to sit around doing nothing, even if you wanted to,' she conceded, closing her eyes as his fingers dipped between her legs. 'I admire your sisters so much. I don't think I would've progressed as far and as quickly as I did at Miss Amore without their attitudes to inspire me—honestly, the number of times and situations where I've doubted myself is ridiculous, and all it needed to snap me out of it was to imagine Blanca strutting around a courtroom like a dog with an ankle in its teeth or think of Carlota spending hour after hour patiently brushing away at millennia-year-old soil to find a fragment of pottery.'

He nipped at her ear and slipped a finger inside her heat. 'No more family talk. I don't want to think about my sisters when I'm seducing you.'

'Is *that* what you're doing?' she asked huskily, even as the pleasure of what he was doing to her was filling her with heated sensation and had her wriggling her bottom against his rock-hard arousal again.

He growled and moved his hand off her breast to pull his shorts down and release his erection.

'*Excuse* me,' she said primly, pulling his pleasuring hand away and darting out of his orbit. 'But I thought you brought me out here so I could swim?'

Shrugging off her kimono, she threw him a wicked grin over her shoulder and then ran, naked, to the swimming pool and jumped in.

The water was wonderfully refreshing, but there was no time to consider this for Xavi dived in beside her, grabbed her legs and pulled her under. Spluttering and laughing, she resurfaced, only to be enveloped in his arms. A moment later, he had her pinned to the side of the pool. They were both still laughing as he dived into *her*.

Movement woke Beth from a deep, sated sleep. Or was it sound that had woken her? The room was dark, but the bed was empty.

She sat up and strained her ears. The shower was running.

Reaching for her phone, she checked the time. Five a.m. What was he showering for at this unholy hour? He could have had only a couple of hours' sleep.

She must have dozed off again because when she next opened her eyes, Xavi was sat on the edge of the bed, fully dressed in a suit and tie.

'You're working today?' she asked sleepily as she tried to blink herself back into full consciousness.

'Back-to-back meetings.'

She shuffled over and put her head on his lap. 'I didn't think you were working again until after the honeymoon.'

He ran his fingers through her mussed hair. 'I'm taking six days off for the wedding and honeymoon. I can't take any more, not with the buyout of the Grimaldi brand.'

She tried not to let resentment stab her. It shouldn't bother her that Xavi was only carving out five days in his schedule for their honeymoon on his family's Caribbean island. She had the feeling he thought she should be grateful for that! He'd mentioned a couple of times about the Grimaldi buyout and how it had dragged on longer than anyone had anticipated. At some point in their near future, he'd be flying out to New York to oversee its push over the line.

What she *was* grateful for was the reminder of where she lay in his priorities: as a vessel to sate himself with in the evenings when the working day was done, a state of affairs she was determined to change.

She nuzzled her cheek farther up his thigh to his groin, then nuzzled her face between his legs, smiling at his arousal.

Lifting her face, she worked at his trousers button,

only to be foiled from opening it by his hand covering hers and moving it away. 'Later. I don't have time now.'

She rolled onto her back and pulled the sheets off her breasts. 'There won't be a later. I'm staying at the hotel tonight.' At the same hotel as her friends and family for one last send-off to the single life.

There was a flash of hunger in his stare, and then the switch turned off.

It was the same switch he'd turned off when he'd ended them.

'We have our whole lives to make love, *mi vida*,' he said reasonably but with an edge to his voice that demanded no argument. He pressed a firm kiss to her mouth, unceremoniously removed the arm she hooked around his neck and got to his feet. Looking down at her, his tone gentled. 'We're not kids anymore, Beth. I have responsibilities, but when we go away...' His gaze dipped down to her exposed breasts and then roved back to meet her stare. 'I promise you will have *all* my attention.'

She never got the chance to reply for he strolled to the door, only looking back once he'd opened it. He gazed at her with an expression that made her heart catch. 'Until tomorrow.'

'Until tomorrow,' she echoed.

He pressed his fingers to his lips and then walked out of the bedroom.

When the door closed, Beth swallowed a breath and closed her eyes, willing the burning tears back.

She shouldn't let him hurt her. He'd already set his markers out and made it clear their relationship would be different to how it had been before. Just because he'd made love to her in such a carefree way on the roof terrace didn't mean his thoughts on the matter had changed.

Just because she'd seen the young man she'd fallen in love with all those years ago reemerge for a brief moment in time didn't mean he would be prepared to let him out again.

For a brief moment in time, she'd felt like she was eighteen again.

She pinched the bridge of her nose and took a deep breath.

All these years of being unable to cry, and in the space of twelve hours her tear ducts had proved they'd only been in hibernation.

She wouldn't let the tears fall. Not for him. Not again.

That afternoon, Beth had barely left Xavi's driveway when her phone rang. It was Paul Haldron, now listed in her contacts under the name of Arsehole. It was a moniker he'd earned and more than deserved. She checked the intercom between her and the driver was switched off, and took a deep breath before answering with a cool, 'Hi, Paul.'

'Beth!' he exclaimed as if they were old friends. 'Just checking in to see if there's been any movement.'

'Nothing since we last spoke.' She saw no reason to tell him things were likely to proceed quicker than anticipated, mainly because his voice made her skin crawl and so she wanted him out of her ear as soon as possible. Everything was in hand as she'd demanded. The granting of probate would release investments and cash assets that would comfortably cover the agreed price.

The remainder would more than comfortably cover the other shares she'd already instructed her legal and finance team to vacuum up as soon as funds allowed. Even after her share-buying spree, she would still have more money than she'd know what to do with.

'Okay, well, keep me updated, yes?'

'Sure.'

'I'm travelling to Europe on business next month. Let me take you out for dinner?'

'Considering my emphasis on discretion, I don't think that's appropriate, do you?' His chuckle made her lips twist in distaste. 'I'm getting married tomorrow, Paul. Don't make any further contact until you hear from me or my people.'

She ended the call and closed her eyes.

This time tomorrow, she would be a married woman. Married to Xavi. Sunday morning, they would fly to his family's Caribbean island where they would make love like rabbits on heat.

Everything was proceeding exactly as planned.

She just wished her heart didn't feel so heavy, and when her phone buzzed with a message, wished it didn't leap with hope that it would be from Xavi.

It was from her father, letting her know they'd landed. She messaged him back saying she'd meet him at the hotel. A moment later, it buzzed again. Again, it wasn't a message from the man who'd spent the night making love to her.

It would never be from him. Not in working hours. He'd set out his markers, and he would stick to them until she broke his defences and control. Five days in the Caribbean should do the trick. If he took his laptop with them, she'd 'accidentally' throw it in the sea.

It was her own control she was having concerns about. She kept replaying their night together and chastising herself. She should have played it like a cucumber when he'd spoken about his past lovers, but she'd been powerless to stop her jealousy seeping out. When she took the company from him, she wanted to be as controlled as him. She wanted to look him in the eye and not display a flicker of emotion. She wanted him to look in her eyes and know he'd been played and that she felt nothing for him.

She only wished it could be the truth.

CHAPTER EIGHT

Xavi rubbed his exhausted eyes and closed his laptop. That was it. The Grimaldi buyout would be finalised the week after his return from the Caribbean. All business was done for the next six days. He would be contactable in the event of an emergency, of course, and he had a couple of video conferences lined up, but they couldn't be helped. His father had worked during family holidays. Xavi and his sisters hadn't thought twice about it...although he seemed to remember his mother pursing her lips when he was late joining them for a meal or activity because of it.

His father had been on the verge of stepping into the role Xavi now held. The Rosbel Group founders had been preparing to embrace retirement when he'd received his diagnosis. Overnight, everything had changed. Retirement plans were put on ice as a miracle that never came was sought.

Strange how prominent his father had become in his thoughts in recent weeks. He was always in his heart, of course, but since Raul's death, he'd pushed himself to the very edge of Xavi's consciousness; a spectre watching his every move.

He'd been five, maybe six, the first time his father had taken him to the Rosbel Group headquarters. As young as he'd been, he'd recognised the respect and deference all the many, many people who worked there had shown him. Xavi remembered how his chest had puffed up with pride that Javier de la Rosa was *his* father, and hoped that if his father was watching and looking over him, that he felt an ounce of that same pride.

He would give anything for him to be there to witness his wedding.

Xavi waited until he was being driven home before calling Beth. It disturbed him how he'd had to stop himself calling her numerous times that day. It had been hard enough putting her from his mind to concentrate on his work while she'd been back in England, but knowing she was here, in his city, and with the thrills from their lovemaking still alive in his veins... *Dios*, he could still hear her laughter as she'd climaxed in the swimming pool.

He'd forgotten how much fun sex with Beth could be. Forgotten how intoxicating that could be.

Putting her from his mind had been close to impossible.

The Xavi of old would have locked his office and video called her.

Just to hear her cheerful, 'Hi, Xavi,' was enough to ease the tightness he'd barely been aware of forming in his chest.

'How are things?' There was a lot of background noise on her side.

'Bonkers. I didn't realise you'd booked the entire

hotel for our wedding. My grandmother, who considers more than half a glass of wine with her Sunday dinner as binge drinking, is currently doing shots with Benoît Blanchet.'

'The creative director of Kovoski?' Xavi had steered the buyout of the Kovoski brand a year earlier and paid a small fortune to the hugely flamboyant and hugely talented Benoît to extend his contract with them.

'The one and only... And Gustav Blanc's just joined their party. Oh, dear. The bar staff are pouring them what looks like flaming sambucas.'

He grinned. He'd only met Beth's grandmother once, when Beth had impulsively whisked him off to England for a long weekend to meet her family. Her grandmother could have come from the central casting version of what a grandmother should be. To imagine her drinking shots with the temperamental Benoît and the normally ice-cold fashion editor Gustav Blanc was beyond his imagination, which reminded him that Gustav's birthday party was coming up soon, and being hosted in Madrid. Xavi disliked Gustav, but the man was powerful in the fashion world and needed to be courted. 'Is everyone else behaving themselves?'

'Only my father. He's gone to bed. He's terrified he's going to screw up our walk down the aisle and thinks lots of sleep will stop that happening.'

'And you? What are you doing?'

'Drinking wine with friends and keeping an eye on my grandmother.'

He came within a whisker of asking if those friends included men. He'd seen the guest list she'd provided and was certain a number of the men on it were men she'd posted pictures of herself drinking with.

Xavi had told Beth he didn't care about the men she'd been with while they'd been apart, but it had been a lie. He knew he shouldn't care. Knew he had no right to care. But he did. He always had.

'How are things your end?' she asked. The background noise had diminished. He guessed she'd moved somewhere quieter. 'Finished working yet?'

'All done and on my way home.'

'Good. You work too hard.'

'For the next six days, I belong only to you.'

'I'm going to hold you to that.'

He laughed. 'I wouldn't have it any other way.'

'You won't be given a choice. I'm not taking any clothes with me on our honeymoon. Only bikinis.'

He groaned softly at the memory of Beth in a bikini. 'I'm tempted to say let's skip the wedding and go straight to the honeymoon.'

'But then I'll miss the pleasure of seeing your reaction to my wedding lingerie.'

'Is it sexy?'

'*Very* sexy.' She lowered her voice. 'I'm still debating whether to bother with the knickers.'

His groan was louder.

'And with that thought, I shall bid you good-night.'

'You're saying goodbye to me now, when you've just made me hard?'

'Have I?' she asked innocently.

'You know you have, you tease.'

Her voice lowered even further. 'Remember how we used to have video sex?'

'You're trying to kill me.'

She laughed huskily. '*Beunas noches*, Xavi. Sweet dreams.'

'*Beunas noches, mi vida.* Dream of me.'

There was a long passage of silence before she softly said, 'Always.'

She disconnected the call.

His heart as swollen as his cock, Xavi threw his head back and laughed.

Beth put her phone back in her bag, rested her hand against her thumping heart and willed the burn between her legs to ease enough to enable her to walk back into the hotel bar without anyone wondering what was wrong with her.

For a few beautiful moments, it had felt like she'd slipped back in time to an age when her love and desire for Xavi had been the purest emotions on this earth.

'Beth!'

She looked at her grandmother, who was half hanging off her stool. Her grandfather was hovering protectively close by. His bemused yet indulgent expression suggested this wasn't the first time he'd seen his wife let her hair down like this, and she felt such a wave of tenderness for them it was almost a physical pain. In their quiet way, they'd taken real, loving care of her when she'd returned to England after Xavi and the baby. They hadn't asked her any questions, just given her the unconditional support and love she'd needed to pick herself up. Her father had been the same, and it was this loving support that had allowed her to put his lies about her mother's family behind her. All three of them had rallied around, and when she'd announced she was moving to Manchester, they'd rallied again to help her.

Their lack of surprise at her sudden announcement years later that she would be marrying Xavi was something she chose not to think about.

What was harder not to think about was the growing ache in her heart for their marriage to be real.

The ache was a ghost from her past, a ghost of the young woman who'd loved him with the whole of her heart and had been loved back with what she'd believed to be the whole of Xavi's heart.

Xavi had to hold himself still. He wanted to pace the cathedral, preferably by the entrance so he could assure himself of his bride's arrival.

The cathedral was packed. Outside, the press had gathered en masse. The wedding of the century was minutes away. All they needed was the bride.

He checked his watch again. She was now officially late.

'Your grandmother was fifteen minutes late for our wedding,' his grandfather said with quiet knowing.

'Yes, you said… You're sure you have the rings?'

His grandfather patted his top pocket.

Not until he'd been deciding on a best man for himself had Xavi considered that he didn't have a single close friend. He had friends. Lots of them. He received regular invitations to parties and nights out, some of which he accepted. But close friends? Not in years.

When had he let his social group slip away from him and become so solitary that he could think of no one to act as a natural fit to the role of best man? He'd briefly flirted with asking Carlota or Blanca to take the role but hadn't wanted to deal with the inevitable fallout from the one not asked.

The natural fit had been right in front of him. Who better than his grandfather, one of the original halves of the Rosbel Group, to hand over the rings as the de la Rosas and Belmontes became more than friends and business partners and became family?

He liked to think it was a decision—and a wedding— his father and Raul would approve of.

It was the change in atmosphere that alerted him to the bride's arrival.

Holding her father's arm, she emerged bathed... shimmering...in light.

All the breath left his body.

Clutching a posy of pink and white flowers, her glimmering white lace dress clung to and accentuated her curves. Strapless, it fitted like a heart-shaped hourglass to her thighs before spreading out like a mermaid's tail, trailing gently behind her. Her auburn hair, swept over her left shoulder in soft waves, shone and sparkled, and as she walked slowly towards him, a lock of her fringe fell into her eyes. Without tearing her gaze from his, she blew it away before her lips formed their dazzling upside-down heart.

Only the roar of blood in his ears told Xavi his heart was still beating.

* * *

Beth had never had to consciously think about walking, but with her legs like jelly, it was taking all her concentration to put one foot in front of the other. There was a tempest of nerves in her stomach, the racing of her heart enough to put a hummingbird's to shame.

Only her father's steady presence beside her kept her vaguely rooted in reality. This didn't feel real. She'd spent the morning feeling like she was in a waking dream and, walking through this magnificent cathedral with its impossibly high frescoed ceiling and with the light flowing through the stained-glass windows bathing everything and everyone in colour, that dreamlike sensation only grew stronger.

It wasn't until she was ten paces from Xavi, darkly gorgeous in a light grey three-piece wedding suit, that the dream veil lifted.

Her hummingbird heart sighed and wrenched in a single motion, and in the next beat, the tempest in her belly churned with such violence she feared she was going to be sick.

She was on the cusp of marrying Xavi.

She was about to wilfully pledge her life to him knowing her pledge was a lie, and as all her thoughts and emotions collided, the impulse to turn on her tail and run away was almost stronger than she could bear.

Her heart wrenched again. She wanted it to be real. This wedding. Their marriage. The old dream of spending her life with him… She was about to touch it. Touch that dream and then step into it. If she could only forgive the devastation he'd wrought on her, she could step into it and embrace it.

Did it really matter that Xavi's reasons for marrying her now were so different to when they'd made their plans for marriage and a family all those years ago? He would be hers, just as he'd once sworn he would always be. Why should she care that he wasn't marrying her for love? He wanted her and desired her; that hadn't changed. Why couldn't it be enough for her when the truth was she'd never felt a moment of real, true happiness without him?

She barely felt her father release her arm or the kiss he placed on her cheek. Her hand had been enveloped in Xavi's, and he was all she could see and feel.

The dreamlike sensation cloaking her again, she gazed into his dark brown eyes and felt the warmth and desire blazing from them warm her skin as effectively as his touch.

The two of them saturated with the colourful light filtering through the stained-glass windows, Beth watched Xavi's lips move as he spoke his vows, but her heart was pounding too hard to hear the words as more than a distant whisper.

And then it was her turn, and Xavi's dark gaze held hers as intently as she'd held his.

Squeezing his fingers tightly, she repeated the Spanish vows, flooded with emotions strong enough to burn her eyes with tears that didn't fall, and yet her voice didn't falter...*she* didn't falter. 'I promise to love, cherish and be faithful, in good times and in bad, all the days of my life.'

When the time came to seal their vows, they gazed into each other's eyes one long, last moment before their mouths came together in a tender, lingering caress that sealed what her heart already knew.

The vows she'd just made...she would never be able to break them.

'Are you happy, *mi vida*?' Xavi whispered into his bride's ear as he moved her around the floor for their first dance.

She turned her cheek from where it was pressed against his chest and lifted her gaze to him. 'I feel like I'm in a dream.'

He smiled and bowed his head to kiss her.

Truth was he felt like he was in a dream, too.

When they'd exchanged their vows, he'd felt something touch him, something that had felt almost holy, which was a strange sensation for a man who rarely attended mass and would have been happy marrying in the grounds of this hotel.

They'd been married only eight hours, but he felt different. He'd felt different since he'd walked Beth back down the aisle as his wife. He hadn't expected that. What was marriage but a piece of paper? It had meant more to him when he'd been young and crazed on lust, and it had felt imperative that he tie Beth to him forever. That young man had let his head be turned for six months into believing in fairy tales and magic. Beth's magic. It had possessed him.

He could feel her spell weaving around him again now, but that was okay. This was their wedding day. She'd made the same vows as he had, to love and be faithful for all their days. Powerful words that contained a magic of their own.

Had he ever stopped loving her? He couldn't say. He couldn't even say if what he felt for her *was* love, and it was dangerous to even think in such terms, a certain path to the madness that had subsumed him before.

He knew better than to let Beth's spell weave too deeply into him.

Tonight he would make love to her all night long, and then tomorrow, they would fly to the Caribbean and make love whenever and wherever they liked, and then they would come home and settle into their new lives together with the boundaries he'd put in place carefully adhered to.

But for tonight and the next five days, he would honour his promise and be entirely hers.

Beth lifted her hair so Xavi could unclasp the tiny button at the top of her dress, and shivered with pleasure as he slowly pulled the hidden zip down to the base of her spine.

She released her tresses as the dress fell into a puddle around her feet.

He buried his nose into her hair and gripped her hips, pressing his arousal against her back. Thickly, he said, 'All day I have wondered…'

Naked except for white silk stockings, Beth turned around and wrapped her arms around his neck. Gazing into his eyes, she whispered, 'Make love to me, husband.'

His molten stare held hers. 'For all my days, *esposa*.'

Her heart, incapable of beating properly the whole of that magical day, ballooned. *Esposa.* Wife. Xavi's wife.

Gathering her into his arms as if she were as light as a small child, he carried her to the honeymoon bed of the honeymoon suite and laid her down.

Their mouths fused.

There was no hot desperation in their lovemaking. Not that night.

Together, they unhurriedly stripped Xavi out of his wedding suit until they were skin to skin. Hands roaming and exploring each other's naked flesh, their tender yet passionate kisses came from the same dream that had carried Beth through the day.

It had been a beautiful day, and she wasn't ready to let it go and for reality to seep back into her psyche.

Let her have this one day and night of believing their marriage was what her heart so wished. One day and night before she pushed the illusion of feeling loved aside and accepted reality back into her heart.

His dark stare locked on hers, he drove into her slowly, then captured her mouth for another deeply passionate kiss.

Limbs tightly entwined and enveloped in a blissful dream of heady emotion, Beth let the pleasure of Xavi's lovemaking saturate her, heart, body and soul, and when she came, consciousness drifted away until it was only them left in the world.

The dream cloaking Beth was still in no hurry to lift itself. She was still in no hurry to shake it off. The de la Rosas' private island was a picture-perfect paradise. Situated between the Bahamas and Turks and Caicos, they'd flown to the former, then speed-sailed on Xavi's new catamaran to the island itself. Barely six miles square, it was thick with greenery and spectacular wildlife and ringed with the finest, softest light golden sand. The shallow turquoise water surrounding it was clear enough for her to swim out and marvel at the colourful fish who'd escaped the coral reefs farther out swimming around her. Even the villa was a delight, in part because it was no villa but a hamlet of Balinese-style lodgings dotted around a main house that had all the facilities of a luxury hotel.

She would have loved her time there no matter the company, but sharing it with Xavi sealed its perfection.

These had been the best days of her life.

'When can we come back?' she murmured on their last evening as they lazed in bed after making love. Her cheek lay on his chest. The comforting rhythmic beat of his heart lay beneath her ear. The French windows of their suite facing the sea were open, a delicious, gentle breeze cooling their skin.

His fingers continued their lazy circular motions on her back as he said, 'As soon as I can carve out more than a few days in my schedule.'

She kissed his chest to stop her mouth from protesting. The dreamlike state she was living in was too wonderful to spoil with words that could wait until they returned to their real life. 'Can we try for the New Year?'

'That should be doable.'

She sighed her happiness and nuzzled her cheek over the fine dark hairs of his deeply tanned chest. A veritable sun magnet, their days there, few though they'd been, had deepened Xavi's olive skin by several shades. By contrast, Beth's pale skin had gained a few extra freckles. She supposed slathering factor fifty sunscreen on every couple of hours didn't help the tanning process, but with her complexion, she wasn't taking any chances. The upside was that Xavi had insisted on being her personal sunscreen slatherer.

'I have to admit, I thought you would find it boring here,' he commented.

'You're kidding? This place is heaven!'

He chuckled softly. 'You're like a bee, always busy, busy flying from flower to flower in search of your next dose of pollen. And you're impulsive. When you get an idea to do something, you jump in with both feet. There's not much scope for impulsivity here.'

She considered this. 'I suppose it depends on where I am and what I'm doing. If something takes my fancy and it's doable, then yes, I'll just go ahead and do it because why hold back? Life is short—we both know that—and so I guess I just want to live it while I can because who knows when it will be over for me?'

He was silent for a long time. 'I can't be like that, Beth. I don't think I'm built to be like that. I have to have lines and boundaries on my time, otherwise everything blurs.'

Her happiness ebbed at the reminder. 'Is this your way of reminding me that our marriage is just a business deal with benefits?' she whispered sadly.

He'd rolled her onto her back before she could snatch a breath; had pinned her wrists to the sides of her head before she felt his fingers wrap around them. 'That isn't what this marriage is,' he said tightly. 'I wanted to marry *you*, Beth. I want to father your children and have a family with *you*.'

Her heart swelled with a combination of hope and sadness, and for the first time since they'd been on their honeymoon, Beth was unable to stop herself thinking about the child they'd lost. The child Xavi had never known existed. Another swell bloomed inside her, a swell of sudden yearning to tell him the truth that he'd already fathered a child with her, but how could she? She'd never spoken the words to a soul and didn't know if she could do it now, and even if she could, what purpose would it serve other than to hurt him?

To hurt him would be to hurt herself.

Xavi was right that she was impulsive. She'd agreed to marry him thinking she was going to embark on a wrecking project to destroy him the way he'd destroyed her, and then jumped in with both impulsive feet on her plan of action to pull it off.

He'd never wanted to hurt her. She was certain of it. Not deliberately. He'd behaved terribly to her, but she needed to find a way to forgive him for that because one thing she was certain of was that she was in this marriage for keeps. She loved him. She'd always loved him. She would always love him. She had no more choice in her love than she had over her natural hair colour and freckles.

The past was the past, and she had to find a way to live with it and find a way to embrace their future together. Find a way to embrace Xavi for who he was and not hate him for no longer being the young man who'd put her first, second and third in his life.

She had no idea how long they spent positioned like that, with Xavi pinning her down, his gorgeous face glaring at her, his arousal slowly springing to life at the base of her pubis.

And she had no idea what he was thinking. The face she'd once read like a book was closed to her of everything but what he wanted her to see.

Without saying a word or yanking her wrists from his hold, she held his stare and tilted her hips so his arousal was positioned at the entrance of her heat.

Neither spoke nor reacted facially as he slid inside her. Neither moved their gaze from the other as he brought them both to orgasm.

CHAPTER NINE

BETH OPENED HER eyes to dusky early-morning light and the weight of Xavi's arm over her belly and the delicious feel of his chest and thighs spooned into her.

She smiled sleepily to herself and wriggled her backside, ready to tempt him into waking and making love to her again before he left her for the office and she collected Diego from Salma. After five magical days away together, reality could wait a little longer.

His arm tightened around her stomach. His mouth nestled into her hair. She wriggled again, luxuriating in the wakening of his arousal against her buttocks, and she turned her head to seek his kiss, only to find the movement hurt her head…and now she realised her head was aching, she realised the weight of Xavi's arm over her belly was constricting and hurting her.

She sat bolt upright without even thinking about it. 'I'm going to be sick.' The words came out with no thought, either, and it was without thought that she scrambled off the bed and threw herself into the bathroom.

She only just made it in time.

* * *

Xavi, propped against the headboard, stroked his sleeping beauty's fevered forehead and closed his eyes.

He'd never known Beth to be sick before. Sure, she suffered menstrual pains—at least, she used to—but that was it. He couldn't remember her even having a sniffle, and it enraged him all over again to remember his doctor's refusal to say whether she was suffering from food poisoning or a stomach bug. He hadn't paid him an extortionate amount of money to drag himself to his apartment at eight in the morning and diagnose his new wife to be rebuffed with *likely this* or *likely that*. He was the doctor. Make the bloody diagnosis and then give her something to make her better, not all this, *either way, it needs to work its way out of her system* crap. Xavi was no doctor, but an internet search had given him a better bloody diagnosis than the so-called bloody expert. If it was food poisoning then Xavi would be suffering from it, too. They'd last eaten on the plane home, both eating the same meal. If it was a stomach bug—much more likely, especially now that she'd developed a fever, too—then that meant some bastard had passed their germs to her. When he found out who it was, he would kill them.

His phone rang.

It was his executive assistant. The head of his cabin crew had just informed her that two of the crew had been struck down with a virulent stomach bug and wanted to warn Xavi in case he was struck down with it, too.

He swore very loudly in his head. He couldn't even

take delight in seeking revenge in his imagination, not when the perpetrators were his hardworking crew.

He did, however, get his revenge on Doctor Do-Nothing by calling him and insisting he pay house visits to both his stricken crew. 'Wear a mask,' he said icily when Doctor Do-Nothing tried to protest.

Beth's eyes opened. 'You're still here,' she mumbled.

'Where else would I be?'

'In back-to-back meetings?'

He smiled at her feeble attempt at a joke. 'I'm staying right here until you're better.' Screw the meetings he had racked up for the day. Some things were more important than work.

He didn't let himself think about the video calls he'd cancelled on their honeymoon. That was a different matter entirely. He'd cancelled one because Beth had wanted to go snorkelling, the other because he'd gone three hours without having sex with her.

'I'm fine. Go to the office.'

'You're not fine. You look like a corpse.'

'You're so romantic.'

'It's a gift.'

She gave a wan smile. 'Honestly, I'm fine. I've not been sick for ages.'

He looked at his watch. 'It's been twenty-six minutes.'

She blinked her surprise. 'Is that all?'

'See, now you're delirious.'

'Now you're a comedian.'

'Another gift.'

'Aren't you afraid you'll catch it?'

'Germs are afraid of me.' And even if they weren't, there was no way on earth he was going to leave Beth alone in this state. Isabel had offered to watch over her but, even though he trusted his housekeeper with every aspect of his domestic life, he was damned if he would trust her or anyone else to look after Beth properly. Besides, Beth was too unpredictable to guess what kind of patient she would make. So far, she'd been obedient, but it had only been six hours of illness.

'I wish they were afraid of me,' she said forlornly.

He smoothed her hair off her forehead. 'I wish they were, too. Now, close your eyes and go back to sleep. When you're feeling stronger, I'll have some plain food brought to you.'

Her smile this time was soft. 'Thank—' The smile dropped. Her head lifted off the pillow, and, covering her mouth, she staggered back to the bathroom.

On Beth's third morning back in Madrid after their honeymoon, she woke feeling much better. She'd made it the whole night without using the bathroom, and the only ache in her stomach was the ache of hunger. Since falling ill, she'd eaten a couple of bananas and three slices of toast in total, and that was just to shut Xavi up.

She didn't have to check his heart was beating. He was cuddled into her, his breaths of sleep dancing into her hair, his warm hand on her hip. She had a moment of wondering whether to wriggle her bottom to wake him, but then thought she didn't want to push her luck. She'd never been that ill in her life. Lord knew how

Xavi had dodged catching it. Maybe he was right that germs were afraid of him.

Besides, she must stink. She hadn't showered in days. Or brushed her teeth.

Creeping out of bed, she dragged her weak legs to the bathroom, scrubbed her teeth to within an inch of their lives, and stripped off her pyjama shorts and T-shirt. She smiled to remember Xavi's insistence that she wear them. 'I'm not sleeping without you, *mi vida*, and I am not going to risk accidentally making love to you while you're ill and defenceless, so let me put them on you.'

How he could *accidentally* make love to her was a conundrum to be mulled over when her brain was fully functioning again. For now, the only thing she wanted to think about was how well he'd taken care of her. He'd given up two full days of his precious work to watch over her. Yes, she was aware he'd worked on his laptop while she'd slept and had often heard his low voice holding conversations, but he hadn't left her. He'd even eaten his meals in the room and insisted they be plain, bland food in case strong scents set her tender stomach off.

Lathering herself, she thought that he did care for her, and though she hardly dared allow herself to think it, that he'd put her over the Rosbel Group must mean she meant more to him than the company did. Or at least put her on a par with it.

'What are you doing?' the voice she so adored chided from behind her.

She turned slowly, her smile forming much quicker

than her legs were working, and was thrilled to find Xavi in all his naked glory. 'Destinking myself.'

He stood beneath the pouring water, closed the gap between them and, his hands firm on her hips, bowed his head to kiss her gently. He grinned. 'Much better.' The grin quickly faded. 'But you should be taking it easy. Are you all clean now?'

'I need to wash my hair.'

'I will do it for you.'

Reaching for the shampoo, he stood behind her and massaged a good dollop into her hair. The sensations in her still-tender head felt heavenly. After rinsing it out, he reached for the conditioner. His erection stabbed into her back the whole way through, but he didn't even mention it, let alone attempt to seduce her. Once the conditioner was rinsed out, he turned the shower off and enveloped her in a huge, fluffy Egyptian cotton bath towel.

'Back to bed,' he ordered firmly, even though his erection was now trying to stab her stomach.

'My hair's still wet.' It was still dripping.

Guiding her to the bathroom chair, he patiently and gently towel-dried her hair as best he could before nodding. 'That will do. Now back to bed. I will have food brought up for you.'

'Can I have scrambled eggs and toast?' she asked once she was settled and Xavi had propped a load of pillows behind her back and head.

'Can you manage it?'

'I think so...but I will only try if you go to work.' It was Sunday but she knew he had lots of stuff to catch up with, stuff he'd neglected while looking after her.

He pulled the stern face she'd become so accustomed to these past few days.

'I'm better,' she insisted. 'I just need to build my strength back up, and then I'll be as right as rain.'

He pursed his lips. 'One more day,' he decided. 'If you hold down the food you eat today, I'll go back to work tomorrow.'

She smiled. Her heart came close to exploding. 'You have a deal.'

Beth managed to eat most of her breakfast *and* keep it down. Even better, Xavi continued neglecting his work to snuggle in bed with her and watch a mindless action film. They were halfway through it when Carlota called. After chatting with Beth and satisfying herself she'd come off death's doorstep, Beth gave the phone back to Xavi. When he spoke his native language, it was always at a breakneck speed she struggled to keep up with, but she picked up the gist of the conversation.

'Have I translated it right that Carlota's going to Egypt?' she asked when the call was over.

He stretched back out beside her. 'You have—she flies out in a couple of weeks.'

'How long will she be gone this time?'

'It's a big site, so who knows.'

'Is your mum going to do one of her big family meals to see her off with?'

'Probably.'

'Good. I love your mum's big family meals.'

Putting her cheek on his chest, Beth cuddled into him thinking what a great life Carlota had. Blanca, too. Both de la Rosa sisters had always had complete freedom to follow their dreams. Xavi, too.

During the days she'd been in bed with her sickness, she'd spent a lot of time thinking about the past; old memories she'd never given air to in the intervening years had resurfaced, one of them being the time Xavi had told her of his childhood dream to grow up into a man just like his father. She supposed it had stood out because he'd so rarely talked about his father. Back then, she'd found his reluctance mystifying. Pretty much everything she'd learned about Javier de la Rosa had come from Xavi's mother and sisters, who'd had no such reticence.

Back then, Beth had feared death, but she hadn't *known* it, not like Xavi did. She'd been too young and unworldly to understand how some wounds ran too deep to bring to the surface, and as she thought this, an old conversation with Carlota rose. They'd been playing tennis, Beth and Carlota versus Xavi. They'd had to cheat their heads off to beat him. He'd taken his revenge by throwing first Carlota and then Beth—he'd had to chase her round the massive garden to catch her—into the swimming pool, fully dressed. He'd sauntered back into the villa, whistling jauntily. Carlota had wrung the water from her hair and laughingly sighed. 'It's so good to see this side to him again.'

At Beth's puzzlement, she'd smiled sadly. 'He's not been like this since Papi died. Happy, I mean. It's been so long that I thought I'd imagined how he used to be.' She sighed again. 'I think he felt it was his duty to become the man of the house and care for us, especially those months Mami wasn't herself, but...'

'What?' she'd asked into the silence.

Carlota had shaken her head. 'I don't remember seeing him cry, not even at the funeral. I don't think he let himself. I don't think he's let himself feel many things since then, and now you're here...' Eyes bright with emotion, she'd thrown her arms around Beth's neck and kissed her cheek. 'Thank you.'

'Are you okay?'

Xavi's voice cut through the memory, and she undug the nails she'd unwittingly stabbed into his chest and kissed it better.

'Sorry,' she whispered. 'And yes, I'm fine. Just thinking.'

'About what?'

'You and your family.' She kissed the marks made by her nails again. 'I was thinking about your father and how proud he must be of you all.'

The arm holding her tightened.

'You miss him still, don't you.'

He breathed heavily, then slowly said, 'Very much.' His hand groped for hers. 'It is strange, but I've thought about him more in recent weeks than I've done in years.'

'Good thoughts?'

'Always. He was a good man.'

'I know,' she said softly. 'And I know how hard you tried to fill his shoes when he died.' She knew a lot of things; things she'd forgotten.

Deliberately forgotten?

No, she thought painfully. Not deliberate. Necessary.

Painting him as a selfish bastard had made it easier to cope with the pain of living without him.

'I idolised him,' he said simply. 'To me, there was no better man and no better father.'

She pressed her ear tighter to his thumping heart and squeezed his hand. 'You'll be a wonderful father, too,' she whispered, a realisation that made her own thumping heart swell, because at heart, Xavi was a good man. One of the best. He wasn't perfect, but neither was she, and he always did what he thought was for the best. Best of all, he was hers. Would always be hers.

And she would always be his.

The rest of the day was spent nibbling at a variety of food, watching more mindless action films, playing chess—Xavi beat her three games to nil and even pretended to be a magnanimous winner—and even making love. It had been very gentle, but when Beth fell asleep that night wrapped in his arms, it was with a heart full of contentment.

'I have good news for you,' Xavi announced the next evening soon after he arrived home from work.

He'd found his wife—how he loved calling her that in his head—sipping water and catching the last of the sun on the roof terrace. He'd called her a couple of times that day to check on her—it wasn't a breach of his self-determined rules of home and work separation because rules were put aside for sickness. That was basic humanity. Looking at her now, he estimated that she looked 90 per cent better. The 10 per cent was the weight she'd lost. She would never look anything less than beautiful to him, but he hoped she regained the weight soon. There could never be too much of Beth, and with that in mind, he was having dinner brought up to them on the roof.

She raised a curious eyebrow. 'Which is?'

'Probate has been granted.'

He didn't know what kind of response he expected, but the deflating of her shoulders was nowhere near it. 'That doesn't please you?'

She sighed and tilted her head back. 'Not really. It just feels...' She shrugged. 'I don't know how I can feel pleased about an inheritance that my grandfather had to die for me to receive. It feels wrong.' She shook her head with another sigh. 'His death still doesn't feel real to me. I haven't mourned him properly, and I don't know if that's because I wasn't close enough to him or because of everything that's been going on with you and me, but you tell me probate's been granted and all I feel is guilty that he's left me all this money when I didn't love him enough to mourn him.'

'He wasn't an easy man to love,' Xavi admitted. 'I knew him all my life and worked closely with him for many years, but I haven't felt his death on an emotional level, either. He was a brilliant man, but hard and stubborn in mind and heart. I think he loved you as much as he was capable of loving anyone.'

'Do you think...?'

'What?'

She met his stare. 'That he was gay?'

'What makes you think that?'

'Just a feeling. It would make sense of a lot of things. I came close to asking him a couple of times, but lost my nerve.'

'I never knew him to have a partner of either sex,' Xavi said slowly, thinking hard. 'He kept his private life very private. Your grandmother left him before I was old enough to remember her. I don't think even my grandfather knows why. I suppose it's not beyond the realm of possibility that he was a closet homosexual, but that leads to the question of why he felt the need to suppress it. He worked in fashion, after all.'

She smiled. 'There is that. And it is the twenty-first century. Lots of older men of his generation have felt comfortable coming out and embracing their true sexuality.' She closed her eyes briefly and gave her head a little shake. 'Probably it's one of those mysteries that should be left to lie. He was who he was. Wishing can't change the past. I can't wish the truth out of him or wish him into being a grandfather I can properly mourn.'

Their dinner was brought out to them, a gentle lemon chicken dish served with plenty of fresh olives, roasted vegetables and tomatoes. It warmed Xavi's heart to see Beth dive into it with much of her old gusto, even if she didn't feel ready to have a glass of wine with it.

'Are you ready to talk about the implications of what probate means?' he asked.

Her smile was rueful. 'Sure.'

'It means everything is now yours. I didn't want to overload you while you were ill, but it actually went through a couple of days ago. As your grandfather's executor and your appointed representative, I've transferred everything into your name. There are some things, like his properties, that will take a short while longer to be rubber stamped, but the majority is now legally yours.'

Was he imagining that her face had paled a little?

'A couple of days ago?'

'Yes. On Friday. I've got to devote my time to the Grimaldi deal this week—I'm off for an overnight in New York on Wednesday to oversee the finalisation of it, but in the meantime I'll get my legal team to reach out to yours and get the contracts drawn up giving me the power to act on your behalf with the business, and we can get it all signed when I return...' Yes, her face had definitely lost colour. 'Are you still happy for that to happen?'

She had a drink of her water, putting the glass back on the table with a clatter. 'Yes, yes...although I've been thinking about it, and will definitely be getting hands-on with the business at some point soon, but I'll stick to the creative side and leave the running of it to you.'

His relief that she hadn't changed her mind on their deal was tempered by concern at her pallor. 'Are you not feeling well again, *mi vida*?'

'No, I'm... My head's hurting a little.' She drank some more water. There was a tremor in her hand. 'Did you notify my legal team?'

'As soon as probate was granted.' To prevent a conflict of interest, Beth had hired her own legal team to take care of her inherited assets and deal with her side of the legal formalities. 'The shares and everything else that could be were transferred into your name straight away.'

She nodded, almost absently, and got to her feet. 'Excuse me, but I need to lie down for a while.'

His concern growing, he rose, too. 'I'll come with you.'

She held out her hand. 'No, don't. Finish your dinner and enjoy the last of the daylight. I just need to get my head down for a little while. Probably the after-effects of the bug, that's all.'

Seeing she was holding herself well and that her legs showed no sign of giving way, he reluctantly agreed.

The moment Beth was alone in the room, she called Erika, the head of the legal practice she'd hired, a woman who'd given assurance she would take the lead in all of Beth's affairs. For the money she'd be earning from Beth, she could damn well take an evening call.

'Has the share purchase gone through?' she asked as soon as the brief pleasantries were over. God, she could hear her voice shaking.

'It has—the money transferred this afternoon at four p.m. I've been liaising with your finance team, too, and all the smaller shares you were seeking to purchase have also been completed. My congratulations. You are now the majority shareholder of the Rosbel Group. I would have called you to confirm, but your instructions—'

Beth gave a helpless curse.

Wariness came into Erika's voice. 'Is something wrong? We followed your instructions precisely—'

'You've not done anything wrong,' Beth assured her, swallowing back the rising panic. 'All my other instructions, though...forget about them. Destroy all record of them. Right now. Delete them, shred them, whatever you have to do to memory hole them. I'm not taking over the company. The original shares I received as part of my inheritance, I want my husband to keep control of them.'

'But...'

'No buts. Xavi runs the Rosbel Group, not me. I don't want it anymore. His lawyers will be in touch with you very soon. Cooperate with them, but for the time being, say nothing about me owning the other shares...' She swore again. 'I have a lot of thinking to do. I'll be in touch soon.'

Her head now hurting like she'd pretended it was to Xavi, Beth crawled into their bed and concentrated on breathing to drive the panic away.

What was she even panicking for? she wondered as the panic subsided. Surely, it was better that Paul Haldron and his merry band of thieves' shares now belonged to her? They were out of the Rosbel Group. She'd removed one of Xavi's headaches for him, which was a good thing.

That she was the majority shareholder meant nothing. She couldn't run the company, and she'd been mad to ever think otherwise.

No, not mad. Just blinded by hurt and rage from the slashing open of old, unhealed wounds.

She would transfer half the extra shares she'd bought into Xavi's name, she decided. That would be her wedding gift to him. That would keep everything equal between them. She could call her finance team and set the ball rolling...

No. Not yet. Best to wait until she'd spoken to him about it, and with his head and time full of the Grimaldi deal, best to wait for that to be completed before confessing because it would be a confession. To explain how she'd magically become the majority shareholder, she was going to have to explain herself, and to explain herself meant confessing everything. It meant telling him about the baby. It meant opening up about how badly he'd hurt her when he'd jumped into Ellen's bed.

It meant opening her heart to him and trusting him not to break it again.

The last of her panic vanished. She *did* trust him. Xavi loved her, she knew it in her heart, loved her as much as he would allow himself to love anyone. If she ever doubted it, all she'd need to do was remember the wonderful care he'd given her when she was ill. Given time, he would open his heart fully to her again, too. She was certain of it. He might be angry with her initially, but once she'd explained everything, he would understand, and he would forgive her.

They would forgive each other and put the past behind them.

Feeling immensely better, she was about to get out of bed and set off to find him when the bedroom door opened.

'How are you feeling?' he asked softly, stepping to the bed.

She pulled the bedsheets off to invite him in beside her. 'Better.'

Fully dressed just as she was, he climbed in. 'You are sure?'

She palmed his softly bristled cheek and smiled. 'I've got a bit of a headache still, but I think you've got a cure for that.'

Laughing lightly, he drew her into his arms and proceeded to cure her.

CHAPTER TEN

A FEW DAYS LATER, on the morning of his flight to New York, Xavi quickly showered, shaved his neck, brushed his teeth, dressed and styled his hair. Incredibly early though it was, he should have left the apartment thirty minutes ago, and he left the dressing room fastening his cufflinks...

'Don't tell me you were planning to leave without saying goodbye.'

He stopped short and turned his head.

Beth was sitting on one of the window ledges, the last of the moonlight pouring on her. She was wearing her silk kimono dressing gown, her glorious hair mussed from their night of lovemaking. It was all that lovemaking that had made him oversleep.

'I thought we said goodbye last night.'

She smiled seductively and beckoned him with a finger.

He closed his eyes briefly as he prayed for strength. '*Mi vida*, I'm already running late.' If they had to take a later flight slot, he would be lucky to make it to the meeting with the Grimaldi executives on time. There had been last-minute hitches to the deal he needed to personally fix.

'Too late to give your wife a final kiss goodbye?' she said in such an innocent voice that he knew before he looked back at her that he was making a mistake.

The smile still playing on her lips, she slowly peeled her kimono open and exposed her naked body to him. Batting her eyelashes, she cupped a weighty breast. 'Sure you won't give me a kiss goodbye?'

He groaned, part with frustration, part with desire. *Dios*, she was irresistible, but he was already late…

She spread her legs and raised her thighs.

Arousal, already fighting his willpower, punched its way through his resistance.

His trousers were undone and he was with her in three strides.

He was freeing himself as their hungry mouths came together, his tongue diving into her mouth as he pressed the tip of his erection between her legs. In moments, he was inside her slick heat, thrusting hard, her wanton moans of pleasure and encouragement feeding him, lost in the exquisite sensation of Beth. He sensed her climax building and drove harder and faster into her, barely holding on to the thick contractions that pulled him deeper into her ecstasy. With a loud shout, he let go, bucking his release furiously into her in one long, drawn-out climax so powerful, white light flickered behind his eyes.

She laughed softly into his neck before her mouth found his again. 'Now you can go.'

* * *

Xavi did his best to hold on to his temper. It was rare for him to lose it. Rare for him to even come close to losing it.

It was also rare for him to make such a colossal error. Okay, so the mistake hadn't been directly his, but it was a mistake in the Grimaldi contract he should have picked up on much earlier, not on the day they were due to finally sign it. Heads would have to metaphorically roll, but the responsibility was ultimately his.

Taking a deep breath, he called Beth.

'Hello, you,' she said, her voice filled with joyful surprise. 'To what do I owe this pleasure?'

'I need to stay in New York an extra day. Maybe two.'

Her tone immediately flattened. 'Oh.'

'There's an error in the contract that needs to be rectified.'

'What kind of error?'

'One that, if not fixed, will cost us millions.' An error that would have seen the Rosbel Group forking out tens of millions extra to the Grimaldi brand's founders. Xavi had spotted it an hour earlier when he'd been poised to sign it, but had decided to give the contract one last skim read first. 'It will be simple to rectify the contract itself, but we're all going to work through the night reading and rereading it to ensure nothing else has slipped through the net.'

'Shall I fly out to you?'

'No. You'll only be a distraction. Stay in Madrid with Diego.' Raul's dog had officially moved in with them.

Knowing Beth had him for company held back the unnecessary guilt at leaving her behind. 'I'll be back tomorrow or Saturday.'

'Okay.' He could hear the upset she tried to disguise, and tried not to feel resentful of it. If he hadn't been so distracted by his new wife, he'd have spotted the error on his first read of the contract.

For all the vows he'd made to himself and the stakes he'd set out when making his proposal to her, Beth had woven him into her spell all over again, and he, lust-filled fool that he was, despite knowing all the dangers, had allowed it to happen.

Time to reset their marriage to how it should have been from the beginning with immediate effect.

'Do you want me to cancel Gustav's party?' she asked quietly.

He swore under his breath. He'd forgotten about Gustav Blanc's fiftieth birthday party. As the editor of one of the last remaining international high-end fashion magazines to still make a profit, Gus was hugely influential in the fashion world, a man with the power to make or break brands. It didn't matter that the Rosbel Group was sailing so high, keeping Gustav onside was necessary and prudent.

'I'll be back for the party,' he said tiredly. 'I need to go.'

'Call me later?'

'Unlikely. I've got too much on. I'll get Fenella to keep you updated and let you know when we'll be back in Madrid.'

'I can't have video sex with Fenella.'

'Beth...' He sucked in a breath and tempered his tone. She was only trying to lift his mood; he knew that, but it was his constant need to lose himself in Beth that had got him into this mess. 'I can't be distracted with that sort of talk. Keep me in your dreams and I'll be home as soon as I can.'

He ended the call and cursed himself again. Keep him in her dreams? Where the hell had that come from? How was that resetting his marriage to where it was supposed to be? Sweet pillow talk was fine, but talk like that when working?

After stalking to his office door, he yanked it open and barked out an order for coffee.

Then he sat back at his desk, took a deep breath, pushed his beautiful wife far from his mind and re-read the offending contract, praying not to find any further errors in it.

Beth paced the living room of the apartment, holding her phone with one hand and rubbing her queasy stomach with the other, trying her hardest not to take Xavi's irritation personally. It was hard not to, and hard not to feel a painful sadness that the cloak of happiness they'd both been shrouded in had been so unceremoniously ripped away.

He was under huge pressure, she reminded herself. This buyout was a big deal. The business press had been reporting on it and were expecting to report its finalisation at any minute. Delays, no matter how small, always fed wild speculation.

She was letting her brain feed on wild speculation,

another thing it was hard not to do when the memory of Xavi dumping her after a business trip with nights away from her had never lost its vividness.

History was not going to repeat itself. Xavi's irritation at his situation was perfectly understandable, not a portent of anything bad being about to happen.

She rubbed her belly again. She'd been feeling queasy since she woke up, and it was now mid-afternoon. If Xavi hadn't been so short and irritable, she'd have mentioned it. Mentioned, too, that her period was two days late…

The ringing of her phone made her jump, and made Diego, asleep in the corner of the room, lift his head curiously.

'Hi, Erika, is everything okay?' she asked her lawyer, trying to pull herself together.

'All good here, thank you. Just returning your call.'

Oh, yes. She'd forgotten about that.

Organising her thoughts, she said, 'Thank you for getting back to me so quickly. One thing I promised myself I would do with my inheritance was buy my old company, Miss Amore. I want to approach the owner directly, but I can't find any information on him. The company was bought out not long after I started with them. I remember hearing at the time it had been bought by a businessman as an investment, but my investigative powers are clearly rubbish because I can't find anything about him. Or her. I think it must be a shell company or something like it that owns it.'

'You want me to find the owner for you?'

'Yes, please. And I'd like a contact number so I can call them directly.'

'We can make the approach for you, if you wish.'

'No, thank you, I want to do it myself.' It wasn't like she currently had anything better to do with her time.

'Leave it with me. Do you want me to call when I have news or should I wait for you to make contact?'

'You can call me.' No more cloak-and-dagger behaviour. No more going behind Xavi's back. She would never keep another secret from him. Secrets were corrosive.

When Xavi got home, she would make her confession, drag the past into the present and then put it to bed, for good.

She cuddled up to Diego with the very strong feeling that when Xavi got home, she would be telling him he was going to be a father.

Beth's very strong feeling proved right two mornings later.

Fed up of going to the toilet every five minutes to double-check her period hadn't started and unable to bear the suspense a second longer, she'd taken Diego for a walk to the nearest pharmacy and bought a pregnancy test.

It was unequivocal. She was pregnant.

She'd barely processed it when Xavi messaged to say the deal had gone through and he would be home early evening. He'd even added a kiss to the message, which eased the tightness in her chest a little.

While it seemed that all the ducks lining themselves up were ducks from the past, history wasn't about to repeat itself. This was something she reminded herself every five minutes.

What she didn't like to remind herself was that the main reason history wasn't poised for a repeat was the business. Xavi needed her shares. If only for that, he wasn't going to come home and sever her from his life again.

After running herself a bath, Beth lay in it until the water ran cold. She kept stroking her stomach, her heart veering from wild excitement to wild terror.

When had conception happened? she wondered. It wasn't like before. She hadn't come off the pill this time. Had it been her stomach bug that had caused it, when she'd been too ill to take her pill? Could it have happened that quickly? Or had she just been sloppy?

Had she...had she been sloppy because her subconscious had been seeking a way to tie her to him forever?

She pinched the bridge of her nose and swallowed hard.

On Monday she'd book herself in to see an obstetrician. Xavi would want to come with her. Maybe the doctor could narrow the conception date. It didn't matter. What did matter was reassurance that this baby was going to be fine, and that all the conditions were right so that it could live.

It was an assurance Beth knew in her heart could not be made. Life was too fickle and precarious for assurances like that.

She swallowed back more tears.

Xavi would be home soon. He would give her all the assurance she needed, and by sheer force of his will, make her wishes for their baby come true.

* * *

Xavi let himself into the apartment. The door had barely closed when an excited Diego bounded over to run rings around him. And then Beth appeared, ravishing in a halter-neck electric-blue satin dress that plunged in a V to her midriff and fell to her feet. A thin gold belt was wrapped around her waist, hooped gold earrings just visible beneath her loose, gleaming red hair.

He couldn't fail to notice the apprehension on her beautiful face, and knew she was thinking about the last time he'd left her behind when he'd gone away on business. Smiling wanly, he drew her to him. '*Mi vida*, you look beautiful.'

'Thank you.' Her arms looped around his neck, her lips forming the upside-down heart that never failed to make his heart ache. 'You look tired.'

'I'm exhausted.' He hadn't slept in twenty-six hours. A cock-up with the flight slot had seen his plane depart an hour later than it should have done. What should have been a relatively short drive from the airport to his apartment had taken an hour thanks to numerous accidents and roadworks gridlocking the roads.

Her crystal-clear green eyes gazed into his. 'We don't have to go.'

'We do. He's holding it here in Madrid so I can attend.' Though God knew he would give anything to get out of the party and spend the evening losing himself in his beautiful wife, but losing himself in his beautiful wife had already caused enough damage.

He kissed her gently so as not to smudge her lipstick. 'Give me ten minutes to change.'

She nodded and lifted her chin for another kiss. 'Can I get you a drink?'

'A whisky fit for an alcoholic should do the trick.'

Her whole face creased into a smile. 'That bad, is it?'

'It's better now I'm home with you.'

Somehow, her smile broadened. 'Good. And when we get back, I'll show you how much better it is to be home with me and how much I've missed you.'

He went to give her another non-lipstick-smudging kiss, but her lips parted and, with a sigh, her arms tightened around his neck and her tongue slipped into his mouth for a hungry kiss that told him more than any words how much she'd missed him.

For one sweet moment, he returned the hunger because, *Dios*, the nights in the bed of his Manhattan apartment had been excruciating without her.

With great reluctance, he broke the kiss. 'Ten minutes, *mi vida*.'

'I'll bring the drink up to you.'

He put a finger to her lipstick-smudged lips and shook his head. 'We are already late. If you come into the bedroom…'

Her eyes gleamed with knowing, but she stepped back gracefully, laughing. 'Go on, go get ready.'

He swooped in for one more kiss, then bounded to their bedroom, reenergised.

Having showered on the plane, he headed straight to the dressing room and donned a black tuxedo and black bow tie. Polished shoes on, hair swept back, cologne splashed on his neck and cheeks, and he was good to go.

* * *

Beth thought it just as well Gustav's party was being held at Madrid's Club Giroud, an uber-exclusive private members' club a short drive from their apartment. Exhaustion was etched on Xavi's face, although he'd certainly livened up since arriving home.

She'd been to Club Giroud only once before, when they'd first been together. Xavi had taken her there for her nineteenth birthday, just weeks before he'd ended it. She thought it best not to mention that to him. There would be enough talk about their break-up when they got home and she made her confession and told him about the pregnancy. Both pregnancies.

For now, she would hug her news to herself and let him circulate and network with his mind where it needed to be—on the business. Because there was no doubt that for Xavi, this party was business to him.

The birthday boy's stare clocked them as soon as they stepped into the club's vast basement. Embracing them both in that non-embracing way the fashion world did so well, he said to Beth in his thick French accent, 'You look well—I do believe you have lost weight since the wedding. Are you taking the injection?'

'I'm afraid an old-fashioned stomach bug is responsible for the weight loss.'

He waved a dismissive hand. 'Whatever achieves the needed results. You should look at taking it for those last ten or fifteen kilos. How is your grandmother?'

Digging her nails into Xavi's palm to get him to loosen his angry grip at Gustav's thoughtless rudeness, she grinned. Compared to most of the stick insects that inhabited the fashion world, Beth was an elephant. It didn't bother her in the slightest. Xavi loved her curves, and that was good enough for her. 'She's doing well, although I think she's only just recovered from all those shots you and Benoît had her doing.'

His cool face became suddenly animated. 'That we had *her* doing? She drank us both under the table and then did the same at the wedding!' Without a flicker, he readopted his usual impervious pose and turned his attention to Xavi. 'I hear the Grimaldi deal has gone through.'

Xavi's tone was as cool as Gustav's, she noted. 'It has, yes.'

'As you are here, some quotes for the magazine?'

His fingers squeezed hers tightly again.

Sensing he was too angry at the slight Gustav had made about her weight to bother schmoozing the arsehole, Beth cut in with a bright, 'Gustav, it's your birthday party! Surely, you're not planning to work? Let the quotes wait for a day or two.'

He considered this through narrowed eyes. 'And you? Will you grant me a short interview?'

'An interview about what?' she asked, confused.

'You are now one-half of the Rosbel Group and one of the richest women in Europe. You are also young and beautiful and married to this beautiful man. My readers—indeed, the world—will be waiting with avid interest to learn about you.'

She dug her nails into Xavi's skin again. Mercifully, he loosened his hold before the blood supply to her fingers cut off. 'Gus...may I call you Gus?'

He looked taken aback at the question, but then gave a short nod.

'Gus,' she said confidingly, 'if I was going to grant an interview to anyone, it would be you, but I'm a very private person. I've not been raised in the spotlight or ever sought it, so I'd rather keep my privacy and stay behind the scenes, and let our relationship remain one of friends.'

He looked even more startled at the notion of friendship, a startlement that increased when a member of the club's security team tapped him on the shoulder and handed him a note.

He read it, his eyes narrowing before his stare darted to them both with barely concealed excitement. 'Excuse me, there's something I need to attend to. I will find you later. Enjoy the party.'

Once he'd disappeared into the throng, Beth met Xavi's tight stare. 'Don't let him get to you—he's not worth it.'

Dark fury was alive in his eyes. 'He's not, but you are.'

'If you're talking about the weight jibe, then don't worry about it. He probably thought he was being complimentary and doing me a favour.'

'Bullshit. And his comment was bullshit, too. You don't need to lose weight.'

'Look around you. Half—more—of the women here are supermodels. They're the women he sees and works with every day. In Gustav's eyes, any woman over eight stone is fat.'

'Then Gustav's eyes need testing. Those women are nothing but clothes horses, and you're not fat.'

'They're the clothes horses who sell the clothes your brands produce to the public. Thin sells. Fact.'

The dark fury faded. With the whisper of a smile playing on his lips, he leaned into her to whisper, 'Thin sells, but curves are priceless, and your curves are the most priceless of all.'

Her smile turned into a beam.

'And it's our brands, not my brands. You're equal majority shareholder.'

If they weren't surrounded by approximately two hundred people, she would have used the opportunity to make part of her confession, but they were and so she let the moment pass and swallowed back her guilt with a sip of the sparkling water she'd swiped from a waitress when they'd walked in, and as she sipped, Xavi noticed what was in her glass.

'Why the water?'

Because she couldn't tell him she was pregnant during a party, either, she smiled and told a partial truth. 'I'm feeling a bit queasy.'

'Still?'

She shrugged to show it didn't matter. 'It'll pass. Oh look, Griselda's over there.'

Griselda was a doyenne of the fashion world, a true original and one of the only creatives whose company Xavi enjoyed rather than pretended to enjoy.

Soon, they were chatting and mingling, and when Beth escaped to the ladies', it was with Xavi fully relaxed and back to his usual charming self.

The club's basement ladies' toilets were as lavish and ornate as the ones she'd used in the club's dining room all those years back. It smelled delicious, one of the many touches that made Club Giroud membership so sought after. Beth touched up her lipstick and eyeliner thinking she'd have to get Xavi to bring her for a meal here again. They could take a trip to Barcelona and try the Club Giroud there, too. Or Athens. Or Paris. Each one had its own distinct style and flavour, and she was keen...

Her thoughts slipped away when she left the ladies' and spotted a bald, rotund man wearing a red cummerbund with his tuxedo approach Xavi. Her blood turned to ice before her brain connected what her eyes were seeing to the online picture she'd seen of him.

It was Paul Haldron.

CHAPTER ELEVEN

Xavi was generally happy to play the schmoozing game at parties like this. It came with the job and was a necessary evil. He might be an apex predator at the top of the fashion food chain, but those lower down needed to eat, too, and if they weren't fed, they died, and then he would be unable to feed. It was an analogy Raul had imparted many years ago. Occasionally at these parties, Xavi would come across a rival apex predator and engage in the mandatory pissing contest, but secure with his place in the world, his heart was rarely in it. It was only with arsehole predators like the shark Paul Haldron that he took enjoyment from metaphorically pissing all over them.

Far from being an actual shark, the Paul Haldrons of the world were more like annoying mosquitoes trying to land on the real apexes with the aim of biting and slowly killing them. Paul Haldron had tried to kill Xavi. He'd led a consortium of investors to overthrow him. It had been a badly misguided effort, mainly because they didn't have the shares, brains or funding to make a success of it. Xavi had taken great pleasure in squashing them all, even if it had been an unwelcome reminder of how vulnerable his position would be without Raul's shares.

Instead of arranging his face into the usual welcoming smile he gave when being approached, he hardened his stare and drew himself to his full, intimidating height.

'What an unpleasant surprise to see you here,' he said sardonically when Paul stood before him. 'I wasn't aware Gustav knew of your existence.'

'He didn't until twenty minutes ago.'

'Then you shouldn't be here. This is a private members' club. Guests are only allowed if—'

'I know how the guest list works. I got a note to Gustav of my reasons for being here. He read it and added me to the list.'

Xavi followed Paul's gaze. Gustav was watching them from a distance. There was no mistaking his avid interest.

Trepidation snaked up his spine.

He looked back at the American. 'Why are you here?'

'Because I knew you were invited and I wanted to see if you had the balls to turn up given the new state of affairs, and offer my commiserations to you.'

The tension spreading through his veins, Xavi folded his arms across his chest. 'What are you talking about?'

The mosquito smiled a shark's smile. 'Your wife becoming the majority shareholder of the Rosbel Group and kicking you into the dirt. I speak from experience when I say she paid good money for that privilege.'

A pulse was beating loudly in the back of Xavi's head, the tension in his veins turning to ice.

The shark correctly read his expression and bared his teeth. 'So it hasn't happened yet? I did wonder— I've kept my ear *very* close to the grapevine and not even heard white noise.'

His words had barely landed when he nodded over Xavi's shoulders. 'Oh, there she is. She's as ravishing in the flesh as your wedding photos suggested. Still, they do say the most beautiful of the fairer sex are the most deadly. That one is lethal. Enjoy your downfall.'

Beth's feet had rooted to the floor. She knew from Xavi's ramrod stance and the triumphant smile Paul Haldron aimed at her as he sauntered away that he'd told him, and she fought desperately against the hot blood filling her head and the sensation that she was a heartbeat away from her legs collapsing beneath her.

He turned around slowly.

Eyes as glassy and cold as marble fixed on her.

Completely incapable of moving, she fought even harder to keep control of her limbs as he moved towards her with the silent lethality of a tiger about to strike.

He took her clammy hand into his with a smile as cold as his stare and leaned down to brush a cold kiss on her trembling lips and whisper, 'Smile, *mi vida*. This is a party.'

For the next two hours, her hand held tightly in Xavi's, Beth smiled until her face ached. Not a single guest went unspoken to. Xavi laughed and joked as if he was having the best time with the best company, feigning ignorance of the curious eyes darting to them as Paul Haldron spread his poison amongst the party.

Beth did her best to act normally, but with the world spinning wildly around her and the undercurrent of ice flowing out of Xavi through their clasped hands, maintaining her smile was taking everything she had.

It was almost a relief when he murmured, 'Time to go,' before guiding her to Gustav so they could say goodbye.

'Excellent party,' he enthused, clasping Gustav's hand as he shook it, then slapping him on the shoulder as he added, 'I'll be in touch about those quotes.'

She had no doubt that the moment the basement door closed behind them, the room would erupt. And she had no doubt that Xavi knew it, too. They would be lucky to make it until morning before the news leaked to the press.

She was too frightened to check her phone to see if it had leaked already.

Their car was ready for them. Gentleman that he was, Xavi let her get in first.

'Xavi,' she said as soon as they set off. 'I—'

'Wait until we get home,' he interrupted tonelessly, turning his face out the window.

'I'm sorry,' she whispered. 'I was going to—'

'Stop the car,' he said abruptly into the intercom. 'I want to walk.'

The car stopped.

He faced her.

His expression made her insides shrivel.

'I will meet you at the apartment.'

He'd slipped into the night before she could scramble any form of response.

It could only have taken ten minutes to get back home, but they were the longest ten minutes of Beth's life. The wait for the elevator was excruciating. The fact she had to call it down meant Xavi had beaten her back.

Diego rushed to greet her, but other than his welcome presence, the apartment was silent. She crouched down to stroke him and snatch at the needed comfort he gave, the coldness in her chest increasing with the certainty that Xavi had sent the staff to their quarters.

At first glance, their bedroom was empty. And then she heard noise coming from their dressing room.

The world spun on its axis to find three open suitcases on the long velvet dressing stool, and she pressed her back against the wall to stop herself swaying.

He didn't break his stride at her appearance, pulling a load of summer dresses off a rack and folding them as one and placing them, coat hangers and all, in the nearest case.

'When were you going to tell me?' he asked silkily as he pulled more dresses off the rack.

She could hardly speak through the hammering of her heart. 'Tonight.'

'You don't need to lie anymore, Bethany.'

She didn't know what was worse, the way he was systematically packing her out of his life, that he'd called her by her full name or the normality of his tone.

'I'm not lying.'

'What percentage of the company do you own?'

'Fifty-one. But—'

'I'm impressed. That was quick work. I assume you had everything ready to go as soon as probate was granted?'

'Yes. I—'

'It did cross my mind to increase my shareholding a few times before your grandfather died, but I didn't act on it—it would have felt treacherous.' He zipped the first suitcase shut and lifted it onto the floor. 'Our grandfathers took great pride in their partnership being equal. Neither could benefit without the other benefiting, too. For me to increase my shareholding while Raul was alive would have spat on that fundamental agreement as it would have made me the first amongst equals. When he died, again I could have increased my shareholding, but instead I went to Raul's granddaughter.' Back at the shelves and racks of her clothes, his gaze caught hers for a moment before he gathered a pile of her jumpers into his arms.

That moment was enough for her insides to shrivel all over again. 'I'm sorry. I *was* going to tell you tonight, I swear. Whatever Paul told you about my motives... they changed. I set the wheels in motion to get majority control and kick you off the board the day after you proposed. I was angry and emotional, and I acted rashly, but I swear, I've no intention of going through with it. I would never take the company from you.'

She might as well have spoken to the wind. Xavi continued his monologue as if she hadn't even opened her mouth.

'I thought we could continue that long-established partnership with us both benefiting equally.' He placed an armful of her jeans and trousers into a case. 'I would continue to run the company and you could slot into it in whatever creative capacity you wanted, and we would both reap the rewards, and—'

'And that will still happen,' she promised beseechingly. 'Nothing's changed there, Xavi. Nothing.'

Her words fell on deaf ears, Xavi picking up exactly where he'd left off. 'And if we were going to be partners in business then we should be partners in life, too, and do that thing we'd promised we would do when we were too young to know what we were doing and finally get married.' Crossing the floor to add another pile of jumpers into the suitcase, his stare caught hers again. His lips formed a snarl. 'It never crossed my mind that Raul's granddaughter would be so treacherous as to work directly against me and stab me in the back.'

Although anger had been bubbling beneath his veneer of normality, to witness it rise to the surface made tendrils of her own anger unfurl.

'That is some major revisionist history,' she defended herself shakily. 'You married me first and foremost to keep control. Everything else was secondary, including your wish to marry me.'

His glare was full of contempt. 'I never lied to you, not once, whereas everything you've done has been a lie.'

'Never lied to me?' A sudden burst of fury propelled her from the wall to cross the dressing room floor and wrench the jumpers from his arms. She hurled them to the floor. 'You promised you would love me forever,' she cried. 'What was that if not a lie? You promised there would never be anyone else for you, another lie, and then you threw me away as if I never meant a damn thing to you.'

But this only made his visible anger turn darker. 'So this has all been *revenge*? All these years and you've been harbouring *revenge*?'

'You broke me, Xavi. You didn't just break my heart, you broke *me*. You threw me away like an unwanted toy without any warning, and then days later jumped into bed with Ellen.'

He kicked a jumper so hard it flew through the air and landed on the far wall. 'I told you before, I never slept with her! Nothing ever happened with Ellen.'

'She sent me a time-stamped photo of you asleep in her bed three days after you dumped me!'

'I don't care what she sent you. Nothing happened. She had a party at her house, and I went along and drank a bottle of whisky and passed out. I was so drunk I didn't know it was her bed until I woke up the next morning to find her sharing it.'

'Then why didn't you say that when I asked? Why lie?'

'The question was about sex, not sleeping arrangements. I never had sex with her. I could have told you I'd passed out in her bed, but I was trying to convince you to marry me, not rake over poisonous old ghosts. Hell, Beth, don't you think ending our relationship affected me, too? Ending us almost damned near killed me.'

She threw her hands in the air and laughed bitterly.

'Oh, I've heard everything now. You were like a freaking robot with its humanity wiped out.'

'And why do you think I had to be like that? It's because it was the only way I could do it—I *had* to switch myself off. My brain knew it had to be done but my heart didn't want to let you go, and I only went to that damned party to drink myself into oblivion so I could try and forget you.'

'You didn't need to forget me! I was at my grandfather's praying to every deity in existence for you to come back to me!'

'We were over, Beth! I wasn't going back to you. Ending us hurt us both, but it was necessary, and for you to hold on to your resentment over it for all these years is just warped when you moved on long before I did. Even if I had screwed Ellen that night, that doesn't excuse what you've done. You married me under false pretences for revenge so you could take control of the business for yourself and push me out, and all for something you thought happened that didn't happen eight years ago?' His face twisted with loathing. 'You sicken me. Take your cases and get out of my home, and prepare yourself for a fight because I am not going to let you get away with your treachery.'

'You don't seriously think I did all this because of *Ellen*, do you?' she demanded, angry heat suffusing her from the roots of her hair to the tips of her toes.

'Who knows what goes on in your twisted mind. You brought her up, not me.'

'As an example of what I believed was another of your lies, but it changes nothing else and it doesn't change what you did to me, and all that crap about you drinking yourself into oblivion because of how much you were missing me? Utter bullshit. If you'd felt a fraction for me of what I felt for you, you would never have let me go. You didn't even try to keep us together, just excised me from your life like you were *ripping off a plaster*, and as for that crap about us being too young to know what we were doing before—I'm only three years older now than you were then! You used our ages and the business as an excuse to get rid of me then, just as you're using what Paul told you earlier as an excuse to do the same now. Look at you, packing my stuff for me and telling me to leave and not even attempting to listen to me. You want me gone, just like you did before, except this time you get to pin it all on me.'

'It *is* all on you,' he snarled, leaning his darkly furious face right into hers. 'You married me to destroy me, and I'm not going to listen to another word that comes out of your lying, treacherous mouth, so take your stuff and get the hell out of my home. The next time I see you will be in court because this is war.'

The room was spinning furiously around her, dizzying her as the truth slapped her around the face.

There was no saving them. Xavi had already been looking for a way out. This was just the excuse he'd been looking for.

All the anger and fight drained out of her as the truth slapped her a second time.

There was nothing left to fight for.

There never had been.

Xavi hadn't played her for a fool. She'd played herself.

Pain gripping her heart in a vise, she stumbled onto the armchair next to her dressing table and hugged her arms tightly.

Her voice was a distant ringing in her ears as she dully said, 'Yes, I wanted to destroy you. I wanted to take your precious company away from you and hurt you the way you hurt me.' Even though her eyes were struggling to focus, she could see the contempt etched on his features, a contempt that tightened the vise until she could hardly breathe. 'I never moved on, Xavi. I never got over you. I tried so hard, but I just couldn't do it. I tried to sleep with other men, but they left me so cold I couldn't go through with it. I've carried you with me every minute of every day since we parted, not just you but our...our...' She had to swallow hard to say it. 'Our baby.'

His head reared back as if she'd slapped him.

The silence that followed was absolute.

Eyes wide, the colour draining from his face, he just stared at her.

'I was pregnant, Xavi,' she whispered, saying the words aloud for the very first time. 'Don't you remember how we were trying for a baby?'

'But...' His voice was hoarse. 'You'd only come off the pill that month. It was too soon...'

She shook her pounding head. 'No. We were one of the lucky ones. It happened straight away for us. I took the test when you were in Milan, and I was the happiest person alive. I was having your baby, the child we both wanted, and that it happened so quickly was, for me, proof that it was meant to be and that we were meant to be.'

He sank onto the dressing stool. 'You didn't tell me.' His voice was barely audible.

'I wanted to see your face when I told you. I imagined your happiness...' Tears were stinging the backs of her eyes, and she fought desperately through their burn. 'I had all these fantasies of how it would play out, but then you came back and you...you...you...'

The tears finally spilt out, splashing down her cheeks in a torrent.

'I thought you would come back to me,' she sobbed, her chest heaving as she drew her knees up to hold herself tightly. 'I didn't—I couldn't—believe you meant it. But you didn't come back, and I lost it five days later.'

He dragged his hands down his face and expelled a long breath. His eyes were shining when he whispered, 'Why didn't you tell me?'

'I would have done, but nature took the decision out of my hands.' After grabbing a handful of tissues from the box beside her on the dressing table, she blew her nose and tried harder than ever to get the rest of her words out. 'When I lost the baby, what could I do but go home to England and try to pick my life up and start again? And I did try, I really did, and I succeeded in many ways, but the pain never left me, and when you made your proposal at my grandfather's wake, it all opened up again. I hated you for asking that of me almost as much as I hated you for excising me from your life the way you did. One minute we were trying for a baby and dreaming of a big white wedding, the next...'

She lifted her hands in the air and flicked her fingers. 'Poof. Gone. You threw me away without even checking if our wish had come true.'

'*Dios...*' It was like he'd aged a decade in a stroke. 'I'm so sorry.'

'So am I.' She pulled air into her ragged lungs and wiped her nose. 'So now you know everything. I agreed to marry you so I could destroy you.' A wave of sadness that was close to unbearable rose inside her. She met his stare. 'I knew when we exchanged our vows that I couldn't go through with it, but I'd already set the wheels in motion. I meant to pull the brakes when we got back from our honeymoon, but then I got ill and...' She closed her eyes and sniffed back more tears. 'By the time I knew probate had been granted, everything had happened. If you want to fight me then fight me, but there is nothing to fight about. I've already set the wheels in motion for half the extra shares I bought to be transferred into your name. It should go through on Monday.' She nearly managed a smile as she locked back onto his stare. 'All equal again.'

Lifting his gaze to the ceiling, his chest rose slowly and deeply.

'You know, since you left for New York, I've had the most awful intuition that history was going to repeat itself, and now it has, in all possible ways.' She took a long breath and gathered what remained of her strength. 'Xavi, I'm pregnant.'

CHAPTER TWELVE

XAVI FELT EVERY atom in his body petrify into a statue. The red-hot fury that had driven him since that shark Paul Haldron told him his wife had been playing him for a fool had turned to static when Beth told him about the child they'd conceived and lost, and now he couldn't think at all. Couldn't move. He felt like he'd been hit at full speed by a truck.

'We never did discuss contraception, did we?' Her sad whisper was barely audible above the white noise crashing through his head. 'Well, I'm on the pill, but for whatever reason, we've made another baby. I guess we must be the most fertile couple in Europe,' she added, her attempt at levity dying as her voice choked. 'So if you are still planning to go to war with me, know you'll be going to war with your child, too.'

Your child, too...

He lowered his shocked gaze to hers. 'You're pregnant?'

Her usually crystal-clear green eyes were red and puffy from crying, but where there had been disconsolation just moments earlier was now...not hardness, he thought distantly, but clarity.

She jerked a nod. 'I took the test this morning.' Unfolding her legs, she dragged herself unsteadily onto her feet. 'I'll make an appointment to see a doctor on Monday and see what happens from there... Can I use your driver to take me to my grandfather's villa or should I call a taxi?'

With the white noise having only reduced a little, he was sure he'd misheard her. 'What are you talking about?'

'I'm going to the villa. It's not sold yet. I guess I'll take it off the market, at least for now, until I decide what to do.' She tried to laugh but failed miserably. 'I don't think I'm in the right frame of mind to make any long-term plans just yet.'

Surely, she didn't think he still wanted her to leave? 'Beth, there's no need to make any plans, not now. The baby changes everything.'

'No,' she disagreed with a sad smile. 'The baby doesn't change anything. We're over. You just made that very clear.'

Had she taken leave of her senses? 'Of course it changes things. We're going to be parents.'

Dios, he was going to be a father. They were going to have a child together, and suddenly he was thrown back to a time when they'd been cuddled up together in the middle of the night, imagining the names they would choose for their children. Why wait until they were older, they'd figured. They loved each other, were going to spend the rest of their lives together, so why not start trying now, while they were young and had the energy to deal with a football team of children? Money hadn't been and never would be an issue...

'Xavi, you don't want me,' she said, cutting through a memory he'd not allowed himself to remember in eight years.

'I've never *stopped* wanting you.' Not ever. He hadn't ended them because there was something wrong with them, but because it had been the wrong time for them. They'd got carried away on a dream that had to wait to be realised.

'But not enough to try and win me back until you got something out of it.'

There was a twisting in his guts. 'It wasn't like that, as I've explained numerous times.'

'Oh, but it was.' She shook her head, her stare becoming distant. 'I used to think you were the most open and loving man in the world, but you're not. It's just a front. You can only give so much, and then you take it all back. You won't make that final commitment—you're always seeking a way out. You used the cock-ups you made with the business and our ages as your excuse before, and this time you grabbed hold of the first concrete reason to weaponise against me and drive me out.'

'You wilfully and intentionally set out to destroy me,' he said tightly, trying to rein in the re-ignition of his temper at the way she was twisting everything. 'How the hell did you think I would react to that?'

'I wasn't thinking. That's the point. I was impulsive and emotional and put wheels in motion when I wasn't thinking properly that I now bitterly regret, but ultimately, even if I'd agreed to marriage with the purest of intentions, the end result would have been the same—you'd have snatched at the first opportunity to end it.'

He grabbed at his hair and gritted his teeth. 'That's bullshit. I understand you're angry with me threatening war with you, but I was angry that you'd been playing me for a fool and had set out to destroy the one thing you knew mattered most to me. I didn't know you were pregnant. If I had, I would never have taken it that far.'

'For God's sake, Xavi, even after everything I've just told you, you've just admitted the business matters most to you, and you wonder why I'm not prepared to stay? What happens if I lose this child, too?'

'Don't say that,' he warned, the twisting in his guts spreading. 'Don't ever tempt fate like that.'

'Do you think I *want* to say it?' she cried. 'Don't you think I'm terrified that history will continue to repeat itself? But I'm the one who lived through it and so I have to mentally prepare myself to live it again, and if it does repeat—and God, I pray on my mother's soul to keep our child safe and let it grow into a bouncing baby we will both love and cherish—then I will be on eggshells waiting for the next time opportunity presents itself to you to excise me from your life. Even if the fates keep our baby safe and it survives, I'll still be living on eggshells because I'll know you're only with me *because* of the baby.

'It might be wishful thinking,' she continued, barely pausing for breath, 'but I think you do love me, you just won't let yourself embrace it. You said your father's death cemented Blanca's serious nature, and I think it's done the same to you—your mother falling apart the way she did forced you into survival mode, and the way you survived was by controlling everything, especially yourself. You're *terrified* of losing control of your emotions, a reason why I think you so rarely speak about your father. You never allowed yourself to grieve for him—'

'Do *not* use my father as a weapon against me!' he raged.

'I'm not! But don't you see—his death affected you terribly and it still does. When I came along, you'd spent years burying and controlling your emotions, putting your family and education and the business first, and I was a way for you to cut loose for a while and allow the fun side of yourself out, right until trouble hit. I was a threat to your control, and so I had to go, and I think the same thing's happened now—I got too close again.'

'No, Beth, you set out to stab me in the back and now you're twisting everything to justify your despicable actions.'

'I'm not twisting anything. You control your working and domestic environment with ruthless precision, but emotions? They're messy and uncontrollable, and I'm not controllable, either. Maybe you'd find it easier to deal with your feelings for me if I was meek and mild and compliant, but I'm never going to be that. I'm impulsive and emotional, and life's too short not to love with my whole heart, and it's too short to waste on a marriage with a man whose instinct is to push me away. I'm not a masochist, Xavi, and I've spent too much of my life hating you to want to spend the rest of it living with that on my soul. I need to let go of the past and look to the future, and you need to do that, too, because our child needs a father who can put them first.'

'How dare you insinuate that I won't put my own child first?' he said savagely. Of all the pseudo-nonsense Beth had just spouted, that burned the deepest. 'The very fact I'm prepared to forgive your treachery and make our marriage work proves I'm putting it first.'

Her mouth dropped open. As if in slow motion, angry colour flooded her face. '*You* forgive *me*? Well, thank you very much. I hope your forgiveness keeps you warm at night.' She stalked to the door, only looking back when she turned the handle. 'You're like a rebooted version of my grandfather. He pushed away everyone he loved, too.'

His heart pumping fury through him, Xavi let the treacherous, backstabbing viper go.

Not until Beth let herself and Diego into her grandfather's villa did the grip on her heart let go, releasing with it a sickening swell of pain that doubled her over and brought her to her knees with a howl.

Xavi was in his home office when his housekeeper knocked on the door and poked her head in. 'Your sister's here.'

He didn't look up from his computer. 'Tell her I'm busy.'

'She said you would say that, and said to remind you that she's flying to Egypt in the morning.'

He swore under his breath. Once Carlota flew off, it would be at least a month until he saw her again, probably much longer. 'Let her in. Take her to the living room and give her refreshments. I'll join her shortly.'

Alone again, he carried on reading through the Rosbel Group's share listing, and then without even thinking, clicked the open tab with the headline from two days ago that screamed, *Beth Granger, granddaughter and heiress of the late business icon Raul Belmonte, breaks her silence!*

His heart had already jumped back into his throat before he read:

> *Beth Granger has denied reports that she's taken a majority stakeholding in the Rosbel Group and denies sacking her husband and business partner, Xavi de la Rosa, from his dual role of Chairman and CEO. In a short statement, Ms Granger said, 'The rumours are categorically untrue. The extra shares I purchased were a wedding present for my husband. While I can confirm that we have separated, the shares remain his and he remains at the helm of our great company and will remain there until a time of his choosing.'*

He'd read it so many times and couldn't understand why he kept returning to it.

'Nice smell of alcohol in here,' a voice drawled from behind him.

He whipped his head round and glared at his sister. 'You were told to wait in the living room.'

'Don't take your shitty mood out on me.' Carlota flopped onto the sofa and stretched her long legs out.

'I'm not in a shitty mood and I'm not taking anything out on you.'

'Sure. Can I have one of those?' She nodded at the

open bottle of whisky on his desk. There was an empty bottle of the same brand in the bin beneath his desk.

'Did you drive?'

'Not that it's any of your business, but no.'

'It is my business. You're my sister, and if you want a drink, get yourself a glass.'

'I'll have the bottle, and it's nice of you to remember.'

'What does that mean?'

'That you have a sister and family. You forgot to tell us you'd split up with Beth. We had to read about it on social media.' She held her hand out for the bottle.

He thrust it at her with a scowl. 'I've already explained that. The news broke before I had the chance to tell you.' The press must have got wind of the story before they'd left Gustav's party. When Beth had left their apartment in the middle of the night, a photographer had arrived to witness her jumping into a taxi with Diego. A close-up had revealed a blotchy face with red eyes. Social media had been in raptures ever since.

She couldn't have planned her revenge any better. The whole of Spain—and England, their English heiress a paparazzo's wet dream—had taken Beth's side and spent nearly two days fervently cheering on her actions of stealing his company from under his nose.

Her statement had dampened the cheers but set off a flurry of wild speculation as to why their marriage had imploded so suddenly and so quickly.

'Any explanation for why you've been hiding away from your family and the world?'

'I'm not hiding away.'

'Then why aren't you in the office bossing around your workforce?'

'I'm working from home.'

She took a slug of the whisky. 'I thought you didn't believe in working from home?'

'I do when the paparazzi are constantly dogging me.'

Her eyes narrowed slightly. 'Blanca says to tell you that you're an idiot.'

'Why would she say that?'

She took another slug of the whisky with a shrug. 'Probably,' she said, wiping her mouth with the back of her hand, 'because you've sabotaged your relationship with Beth again. She didn't go into detail, so I'm just speculating.'

'There was no sabotage,' he said flatly. 'Beth was actively working against me from the beginning.'

'That's not what her statement said.'

'Her conscience caught up with her.' Every share she'd bought behind his back had been transferred into his name, not just the half she'd said she would give him. He'd received the notification and felt only betrayal. He'd received her text telling him she'd seen a doctor and that all was well with the baby, and felt such conflicting emotions that he'd opened a litre bottle and buried himself in whisky and spreadsheets.

'Has yours?'

He shook his head in disbelief. 'Don't tell me you're taking her part, too? You don't even know what happened.'

'I don't need to know what happened. I know you,

and I know Beth. She thinks with her heart. You think with your brain.'

'And I suppose you think her heart is as pure as the driven snow,' he said icily.

'I didn't say that.' She smiled beatifically. 'So when are you going to prostrate yourself and beg her to take you back?'

He shook his head again. 'That's just great. You take her part and assume I'm the one who needs to apologise.'

'Like I said, I know you both, but if I'm reading things wrong, then I apologise.' She didn't look sorry. Or sound sorry. 'So why are you sat in your study drinking whisky on a Wednesday afternoon?'

'I told you, I'm working from home.'

'Have you tried sleeping at home, too? The bags under your eyes are bigger than Blanca's handbag.'

'Have you only come here to insult me and put me in a bad mood?'

'I came to say goodbye, the insults are free, but if my presence puts you in a bad mood then I'll consider it a bonus.'

'What the hell is wrong with you?' he demanded. Carlota had always been the more aggravating of his sisters, but this was a whole different level.

'Wrong question, Xavi—the question you should be asking is what's wrong with *you*.' Without any warning, she sat up and leaned forward, all playfulness wiped from her face. For a moment, he saw Blanca in her expression. 'Why would you let her go again?'

Wrong-footed, he swore. 'It isn't as... Look, it's none of your business.'

'You're my brother. That makes it my business,' she

neatly threw back at him. 'You're my brother, and I love you, and it is my duty as your sister to be honest with you.'

'If I want honesty, I'll ask for it.'

'Like my insults, my honesty comes free.' Dark eyes so like his own softened. 'Xavi, you're a great man, in so many ways, and a great brother, too. If it hadn't been for you, I don't think I'd be who I am today. You're the one who got me through those months after Papi died and Mami got lost in herself. You're the one who let me know it was okay to laugh and be happy again, but I don't remember *you* ever being happy after he died, not until Beth came into your life. Those months you were with her... Xavi, you were the happiest I'd ever seen you, and when you ended it, it was like a part of you died. Outwardly, you were normal, but you became insular and you slipped away from us, and I didn't even realise it, not until you brought her back into your life, and it was like... Oh, Xav, you should have seen your face on your wedding day—you were wearing your heart on it. You love her, and she loves you, and whatever happened to drive you two apart, fix it, please.'

'It isn't that simple,' he whispered hoarsely. His heart had swollen and filled his throat.

She knelt before him and cupped his cheeks, forcing him to meet her earnest stare. 'It *is*. Xavi, it is. I spend my life digging through the past, and when I'm working on ancient human remains, the one question I always ask myself of them is *who loved you*? I'll never know, but they would have known because we always know who loves us.

'Do you remember how Papi was when he was ill?

He didn't spend his final days with the business. He spent them with those he loved and who loved him—us, his family. It was *us* he wanted and needed. A business can never embrace you and it can never love you...' Carlota's voice trailed away as water flowed over the hands cupping her brother's cheeks. 'Xavi?'

But he couldn't speak. Couldn't breathe. All these days spent staring at the screen of his computer, veering wildly between despising Beth for her treachery and despising himself for despising her, drinking his conscience to sleep but unable to sleep himself, lying in the bed he'd bought with Beth in the subconscious of his mind and feeling like his heart had been ripped out.

It *had* been ripped out. He'd ripped it out.

He'd broken her again, broken her when she needed him most.

He'd broken them both.

He couldn't contain it any longer. All the emotions he'd spent decades suppressing broke free.

Burying his face in his sister's shoulder, Xavi wept for the first time since he was a little boy.

He wept for the father he'd worshipped and all the years fate had stolen from them, and he wept for Beth and the life she'd lost, the life they'd made together.

He should have been with her.

God help him, he should always have been with her.

CHAPTER THIRTEEN

'ARE YOU SURE?' Beth whispered. Her head was reeling.

'One hundred per cent,' Erika said, sounding almost as dazed as Beth felt. 'Miss Amore is owned by your husband. He bought it eight years ago.'

'But...' It didn't make any sense. How did Xavi own it? *Why* did he own it? And why had he never mentioned it? 'Do you have the date he took ownership of it?'

Erika gave her the date. It was two months after Beth had started her internship there. If she was remembering her dates rightly, it was around the time she'd been offered a permanent contract.

'Do you still want to make contact yourself about buying it?' Erika asked cautiously.

'I don't know what I want.' Her head was reeling too much to think.

Just when she thought she had herself on a vaguely even keel, she was knocked for six again.

The call over, she stroked under Diego's ears in the way he so liked, remembering that morning when she'd walked into the dining room and found Xavi stroking Diego in the same way.

In the four days they'd been apart, she'd received one

message from him. It had been a response to her message after she'd seen the doctor and confirmed that all was well with the baby.

Thanks for letting me know—it's appreciated. Please let me know when you book the scan.

And that had been it.
Excised again.
Except this time the excising had come from her. She'd been the one to walk away.

She wished it made her feel better about things, but it didn't. She wished transferring the entirety of the Rosbel Group's shares she'd bought into Xavi's name made her feel better, but it didn't.

Those who said the first cut was the deepest had never lived with the same wound being cut back open with a deeper, sharper blade.

She wished she'd handled it all better from the start. Wished she'd been honest with him about how she felt. If she'd told him all the stuff she'd posted over the years and her bright and happy demeanour whenever she was in his company had been a front, he would have run a mile…

And their baby wouldn't have been conceived, so she retracted that wish.

Who was to say, though, that Xavi would have run a mile? He'd wanted her shares. He would have done anything for them.

He'd wanted her shares, but he'd wanted her, too, and though it hurt her to think it, the more she thought back on their time together, the more certain she was that he loved her, too, which only made her heart hurt even more. She wouldn't have believed there was anything left of her heart to break, but remembering how he'd stayed with her all those days of her illness did it every time.

Feeling tears prickle, she closed her eyes and concentrated on breathing. After eight years of her tear ducts refusing to work, they were making up for lost time with overtime added in. All she seemed to do was cry, and crying was no good when she was trying to plan her and the baby's future.

This pregnancy felt different. She couldn't explain why. It just did. And that made her dare to hope that this time the outcome would be different.

She would stay in Madrid. No running back to England like last time. Her baby deserved to grow up in a city where both its parents lived, even if they couldn't live together. She'd put on a front before around Xavi. Given time, she could do the same again for their baby's sake. After all, she was the queen of fake it till you make it. She just needed time.

Her intercom rang, making her jump.

Bloody paparazzi. They'd been staking out the villa. She'd hoped her statement would be enough to send them on their way, but nope. Thank God for Salma. She'd slipped out and stocked up on food…and here she was, looking troubled.

'What's wrong?' she asked.

'Xavi's at the gate.'

Her heart punched her. She cleared her throat. 'Did he say what he wants?'

'No. Only that he's here to see you.'

Gently pushing Diego off her lap, she got to her feet and nodded. 'Okay. Let him in.'

Somehow, she managed to stagger up to her room. Struggling to breathe, she ran a brush through her lank hair, added a sweep of colour over her wan cheeks and a touch—only a touch; her hands were shaking—of mascara to her lashes.

Looking only a little less like death warmed up, she gripped the banister tightly as she made her way back down the stairs.

She was three steps from the bottom when the door opened, and a tall, lean figure holding a document folder stepped into the villa.

Her foot stopped mid-air. A moment later, Diego went charging over to him.

Beth used the moment he spent petting the dog to put her foot back on the step. It took a conscious effort to do it.

Their eyes met.

She thought she was going to be sick.

Lifting her chin, she wrapped her cardigan—she couldn't seem to get warm despite the heat—across her chest and said in a voice that hinted at normality, 'Hello, Xavi. To what do I owe the honour?'

He stared at her for a long moment, and in that stare she took him in. The unkempt hair. The unkempt beard. The shirt and trousers that looked like they'd been slept in. The bags under his red eyes and the lines that had deepened into grooves on his face.

And he took her in, too, and she knew he was seeing the lankness of her ineffectually brushed hair and the bruises beneath her red eyes.

Terrified she was going to burst into tears, she reached the floor and turned towards the kitchen. 'Coffee?'

'Please.'

With the excuse of fixing him a coffee and making herself a decaffeinated tea from the supply of English teabags Salma had bought her, Beth kept her back to him and filled the kettle. 'So, why are you here? Is it to do with the business?'

'In a way.' His voice sounded as rough as he looked. 'The shares you gave me... I've transferred them back into your name. I know it's unnecessary, but I've printed them off for—'

'*No!*' Her refutation came out as a wail, and she had to squeeze her eyes shut to better control herself. 'Xavi, I don't want them. I don't even want the shares I've got.'

'Then sell them. Sell them all. Do whatever you want with them, they're yours, but before you make a decision, know I've tendered my resignation from the Rosbel Group. An official press announcement will be released at six p.m.'

She jolted and came within a whisker of spinning around to look at him. Her stare flicked to her watch. It would be 6 p.m. in two minutes.

Her legs trembling as badly as her arms, she leaned her stomach into the counter and added a scoop of fresh coffee beans into the machine, except she missed and the beans went scattering over the surface and floor. Charging over to the cleaning cupboard on the other side of the kitchen for the dustpan, she was on her hands and knees clearing her mess before she was able to clear her constricted throat and ask, 'Why have you done that?'

'Beth, please stop doing that.'

'It needs to be done. Why have you resigned?'

He crouched down in front of her and put his hand on her wrist. 'Please, Beth, stop.'

She snatched her hand away, coffee beans spilling out of the dustpan in the process, and shook her head, terrified to look at him, terrified the tears blinding her were going to fall. 'Please go,' she whispered. 'I'm not ready to pretend to be normal around you.'

'I resigned because I love my wife.'

Her whimper at this was so faint Xavi could have believed he'd imagined it, but the way his heart ripped at the sound... Oh, he deserved to be strung up for what he'd done to her.

'Beth, those shares are yours. I could have bought them when your grandfather died, but the reason I didn't had nothing to do with keeping the de la Rosa and Belmonte partnership going like I said—it was so I had a legitimate reason to bring you back into my life. It wasn't the shares I wanted, it was *you*.'

A truth he'd finally acknowledged on his sister's shoulder when the truth had refused to be hidden away any longer under the flood of decades of suppressed emotion that had poured out of him.

She rocked back onto her bottom and drew her knees to her chin.

'I'm sorry, *mi vida*,' he said starkly. 'I'm sorry for everything. All the pain I've caused you. All the pain I've put us both through. All the wasted years. My feelings for you... I have loved you since the day I met you, and I will love you to the day I die. I've buried myself in work all these years, telling myself I'm continuing my father's legacy when all I was doing was selfishly burying myself from the pain of missing you.'

With a deep sigh, he sank to his backside and looked at her, wishing he could touch her, wishing she would open her eyes.

'Losing my father and seeing my mother lose herself in grief broke something in me,' he said quietly. 'You fixed it without me even noticing. You came into my life, this impulsive, vibrant, affectionate redhead, and you healed me, but when I spent that time away from you in Milan and realised the mistakes I'd been making because of my need to just *be* with you, I pulled away from you and then pushed you away from me because I couldn't handle just how deeply in love with you I'd fallen. I had no control over it, and I *needed* control, Beth. You were right about that, as you were right about so much else. I needed to control everything, and with you, I had none. I never have, and I was a fool to think I could bring you back into my life and not lose my head all over again.

'I don't want a meek, compliant wife,' he continued. 'I want you exactly as you are, because exactly as you are is all I need, and I will never forgive myself for the way I ended it with you all those years ago. I should have guessed you were pregnant.' The burn of tears stabbed the backs of his eyes, and he blinked hard to control it. 'I remember those calls we had and the excitement in your voice... I knew you were keeping something from me, but in my arrogance, I thought you had something special planned for when I got back. That's why I broke things off as soon as I walked in and didn't give you the chance to tell me. My analogy of ripping a plaster off was crude and cruel, but there is no better way to describe it, and because of my cruelty, you were alone when you lost our baby when I should have been with you, and thinking of that kills me.' Throat close to choking, Xavi wiped a tear away. He needed to get through this. Beth deserved everything, not half measures. It was the least he owed her.

'I'd promised you forever and I threw you away, and I want you to know that whatever happens between us now, *mi vida*, know you will never be alone again and I will never, ever, discard you again. I will be there for you, in whatever capacity you need. The business is yours to do as you wish. Appoint whoever you want to run it, run it yourself, whatever you want. You're the majority stakeholder. It's yours. I want nothing to do with it. You and the baby are my only priorities now. I'm yours, however you need me and I will be forever.'

He blew out through his constricted airway and wiped away another tear. 'Please, Beth. Please, find it in your heart to forgive me. I know I don't deserve it, but I swear I will do everything I can to earn it.'

Another blow of air, and he dragged himself back to his knees.

She was still frozen, chin on her knees, eyes closed.

He pressed his mouth to the top of her head and breathed her in. 'I love you, *mi vida*. Always. Call me whenever you need me.'

Beth heard Xavi's footsteps disappear like a receding echo. When the last echo vanished, the tears came. Rolling into a ball on the floor, she sobbed her heart out, wishing harder than she'd ever wished for anything that she could believe him.

She *ached* to believe him, just as she'd ached to believe their marriage could be a real one.

When the tears had finally run dry, she sat herself up and hugged her chest, which felt so bruised. Coffee beans were scattered all over the floor, and the ache in her heart stupidly wrenched even harder to know he'd gone without having his coffee.

She could feel his breath in her hair.

She hugged herself, wishing so hard that he'd wrapped his arms around her so she could still feel his imprint on her.

She wished she didn't love him so much. Her heart, her *amor*...

Amor.

Amore.

Miss Amore.

Her heart punched her again, this one landing like a slap, and suddenly she was filled with the memory of the moment her grandfather had introduced them. That very first look between them. The way Xavi's eyes had widened. The way her heart and her breath had caught.

The memory fast-forwarded into a reel of their time together. Oh, how young and carefree they'd been. How *happy*, always smiling and laughing, always touching each other, drugged on nothing but love and desire...

The reel shifted, flying to their ending and Xavi's words when he'd broken them: *It doesn't have to be forever... I'll always care for you and will always be there for you.*

Through the brutality of his other words, those words had faded into insignificance, but now, through the hot blood pulsing in her brain, Beth realised they'd been the most truthful words of all. He *had* always cared for her, through all the years of their separation. He'd never stopped caring. Never stopped loving her, but she...

Foolish, heartbroken Beth, so recently wounded by the lies of her father about her mother's family and the double life she suspected her grandfather of living, hadn't believed it. Not once Ellen's cruel pictures had pinged into her phone.

But the truth had always been there, as clear as the truth of her love for him that had always lived deep in her heart. She'd just been too frightened and heartsick to see it.

Xavi had never stopped loving her,

Still half-dazed, she scrambled to her feet and yanked her phone out of her back pocket.

Miss Amore.

Xavi had bought Miss Amore for her, so he could

always be looking over her. Taking care of her. Loving her.

She scrolled the numbers as she ran to the door.

Miss Amore.

She pressed Xavi's name and ran down the long drive. It went to voice mail as she reached the closed gate. He'd gone.

Ignoring the cameras suddenly flashing in her face as the waiting paparazzi realised their prey had come out to play, she pressed the code to open it and pressed his name on her phone again.

It went straight to voice mail.

Barging her way through the scrum of photographers, she started composing a message to him as she ran, and then her phone rang in her hand.

'Mi vida?'

'Miss Amore,' she burst out.

'Beth?' There was alarm in his voice. 'Are you okay?'

'Miss Amore!' Half laughing, half crying, she said, 'I love you, Xavi. I love, love, love you. I love you to the edges of the universe! I love you, and you love me, and we've lost so many years, and I can't bear to spend another second without you! Please, come back and take me home. Come back and get me, *please.*'

She heard him shout for his driver to turn the car around, and though she knew he would be with her in minutes, still she ran and still she laughed, her heart pounding, overwhelmed with a joy she'd never believed she would feel again, a joy so pure she felt it in the tips of her toes.

A black SUV appeared in the distance.

She ran even faster.

A figure threw himself out and ran towards her.

She threw herself into his arms.

He caught her, just as she knew he would, just as he would be there to catch her, always, for the rest of her life.

EPILOGUE

Xavi rolled over in his sleep. Instinctively, he reached for Beth and pulled himself awake when he found the bed empty. He craned his ears, even though he knew he wouldn't hear her. She woke in the twilight hours every night and was unable to fall back to sleep until she'd satisfied herself that their children were sleeping safely. She would check on three-year-old Javier first because his room was closest to theirs, and then five-year-old Lorena, and then she would slip back into their bedroom and slide back beneath the sheets, as quiet as a mouse.

The moonlight pouring through their window showed the swell of her pregnant belly as she shrugged her robe off. Moments later, she was back in his arms with her head on his chest and her ear resting right above where his heart beat.

He was just dozing back off when she gently pressed his palm to the spot on her belly their baby was playing football against.

Smiling, he drifted back into sleep.

Life was wonderful.

THE END

* * * * *

Did Marriage Made in Revenge
leave you wanting more?
Then you're certain to love these
other dramatic stories from Michelle Smart!

Resisting the Bossy Billionaire
Spaniard's Shock Heirs
Forgotten Greek Proposal
His Pregnant Enemy Bride
Greek Boss to Hate

Available now!

Get up to 4 Free Books!

We'll send you 2 free books from each series you try PLUS a free Mystery Gift.

FREE Value Over **$25**

Both the **Harlequin Presents** and **Harlequin Medical Romance** series feature exciting stories of passion and drama.

YES! Please send me 2 FREE novels from Harlequin Presents or Harlequin Medical Romance and my FREE gift (gift is worth about $10 retail). After receiving them, if I don't wish to receive any more books, I can return the shipping statement marked "cancel." If I don't cancel, I will receive 6 brand-new larger-print novels every month and be billed just $7.19 each in the U.S. or $7.99 each in Canada, or 4 brand-new Harlequin Medical Romance Larger-Print books every month and be billed just $7.19 each in the U.S. or $7.99 each in Canada, a savings of 20% off the cover price. It's quite a bargain! Shipping and handling is just 50¢ per book in the U.S. and $1.25 per book in Canada.* I understand that accepting the 2 free books and gift places me under no obligation to buy anything. I can always return a shipment and cancel at any time. The free books and gift are mine to keep no matter what I decide.

Choose one:
- ☐ Harlequin Presents Larger-Print (176/376 BPA G36Y)
- ☐ Harlequin Medical Romance (171/371 BPA G36Y)
- ☐ Or Try Both! (176/376 & 171/371 BPA G36Z)

Name (please print)

Address   Apt. #

City   State/Province   Zip/Postal Code

Email: Please check this box ☐ if you would like to receive newsletters and promotional emails from Harlequin Enterprises ULC and its affiliates. You can unsubscribe anytime.

Mail to the Harlequin Reader Service:
IN U.S.A.: P.O. Box 1341, Buffalo, NY 14240-8531
IN CANADA: P.O. Box 603, Fort Erie, Ontario L2A 5X3

Want to explore our other series or interested in ebooks? Visit www.ReaderService.com or call 1-800-873-8635.

Terms and prices subject to change without notice. Prices do not include sales taxes, which will be charged (if applicable) based on your state or country of residence. Canadian residents will be charged applicable taxes. Offer not valid in Quebec. This offer is limited to one order per household. Books received may not be as shown. Not valid for current subscribers to the Harlequin Presents or Harlequin Medical Romance series. All orders subject to approval. Credit or debit balances in a customer's account(s) may be offset by any other outstanding balance owed by or to the customer. Please allow 4 to 6 weeks for delivery. Offer available while quantities last.

Your Privacy—Your information is being collected by Harlequin Enterprises ULC, operating as Harlequin Reader Service. For a complete summary of the information we collect, how we use this information and to whom it is disclosed, please visit our privacy notice located at https://corporate.harlequin.com/privacy-notice. Notice to California Residents – Under California law, you have specific rights to control and access your data. For more information on these rights and how to exercise them, visit https://corporate.harlequin.com/california-privacy. For additional information for residents of other U.S. states that provide their residents with certain rights with respect to personal data, visit https://corporate.harlequin.com/other-state-residents-privacy-rights/.